THE
UNREPENTANT

Praise for *The Unrepentant*

"Turning history inside out, Sharmini Aphrodite's *The Unrepentant* insinuates itself into the unseen gaps of national narratives, into the mutable space between the established order and the promised revolution. Dark and elliptical, these stories have the feverish allure of half-remembered dreams."

—Jeremy Tiang, author, *State of Emergency*

"*The Unrepentant* delicately portrays the inner lives of 'Malayan Emergency' fighters who devoted everything to the dream of a better world. Every character in these stories is deeply felt, every sentence intimately crafted. Sharmini Aphrodite's poetically raw writing is simultaneously paean and the tenderest manifesto."

—YZ Chin, author, *Edge Case*

"In stunning, pitch-perfect prose, Sharmini Aphrodite brings to light the forbidden histories of the freedom fighters erased by the official narratives of the Malaysian and Singaporean nation-states. This is a collection destined to become a classic: it will burn itself into the collective memory of the region with its lyricism, its honesty, and its exquisitely keen yet somehow also oneiric rendering of both place and psychology."

—Preeta Samarasan, author, *Tale of the Dreamer's Son*

"These stories document loss, exile, and forgetting as their characters enter the jungle of a Malayan past and vanish from dominant narratives. Yet they also offer hope through persistent rituals of remembrance and rediscovery enacted by those who remain. In *The Unrepentant*, memory transgresses boundaries and enters bodies and landscapes, splitting history open, and offering the possibility of imagining new worlds. Its stories are historically grounded, achingly beautiful, and reveal Sharmini Aphrodite as a path-breaking new talent in Malaysian literature."

—Philip Holden, author, *Heaven Has Eyes*

"Inhabited by voices who find themselves on the wrong side of history in postwar Malaya, Sharmini Aphrodite's debut collection breaks new ground by staking a claim on an internationalist guerrilla mythos for the peninsula. Epic and intimate by turns, *The Unrepentant* is peopled by Indonesia Raya revolutionaries evading the British authorities, a young Chinese man who joins the armed struggle in the jungle, a woman in love with a married party leader, and their future selves looking back across borders and time, unable to return home. Divisions between races and religions run so deeply, that to love a different person or another vision of the nation is to run the risk of dying to one's community and history. Dreaming of an unfractured Malaysia, *The Unrepentant* holds forth the possibility of memory even where no future exists."

—Ann Ang, literary researcher and writer

THE UNREPENTANT

STORIES

SHARMINI APHRODITE

Published by Gaudy Boy LLC,
an imprint of Singapore Unbound
www.singaporeunbound.org/gaudyboy
New York

For more information on ordering books, contact jkoh@singaporeunbound.org.

ISBN 978-1-958652-20-6
eISBN 978-1-958652-21-3

Library of Congress Control Number: 2025938319

Cover design by Flora Chan
Interior design by Jennifer Houle

To the few unrepentant
To the new generations

From the dedication to The Labour of Job *by Antonio Negri*

CONTENTS

THE LIGHT
OF GOD

Our brother was going to be the first Malaysian cosmonaut. This was decided in the April of 1961, just after the Soviets launched Yuri Gagarin into space. Our brother was eleven then, and we were six. We did not understand very well what a Soviet was. All we knew, our brother's excitement infecting us, was that a man had gone up there—to whatever existed beyond the sky. This was not a figment of mythology, though it took on the same import in our young minds. The cosmonaut's humanity was something our brother was insistent that we acknowledge, stretching out his forearm for us to pinch, which was one of our favourite games. We observed the red, half-moon pucker of his skin, watched as it faded away. *Understand anot*, he said to us, speaking as we always spoke, in a jumble of language. *Now someone is up there*—his finger moving from his heart to our tin roof—*among the stars*.

There were, of course, the expected difficulties with this plan. The first was nomenclature. In 1961, our brother's plan was to be the first *Malayan* in space. Two years later, when the country became Malaysia, he had to amend that to being the first *Malaysian*.

The other issue was that we lived in a kampung in Johor that was everything at once without being anything at all. To our right was a fishing village that seemed as if it had washed up on the shore from the sea. To our left, beyond a stretch of jungle that inflamed our night-time imaginations, was a rubber plantation. Somewhere beyond all of that was some little town that was nothing more than three rows of shophouses. Its walls were newly painted but already peeling in the humidity. Such were our lives. We were not from Kuala Lumpur or Singapore, where things *happened*. We were not from Moscow, where people and dogs—our brother had mourned the death of Comrade Laika—were plucked from the street and thrown into space at whim to play with the stars. That was the gamble of geography.

So yes, we had no idea how our brother *would* end up a cosmonaut precisely. But despite all this we were sure a solution would present itself. We believed in our brother. After having to leave school, he worked with our father at a mechanic's in town, and everything that was brought to him he could fix. Car, motorbike, four-wheel drive—anything, whatever, boleh. He was a charmer of aunties and young women alike. And, most importantly, he was our brother—who had saved us from being eaten by a baby buaya when we were ourselves babies, who had saved us from drowning each other when we were a little older, who had saved us from our mother's many kicks-and-slaps by offering his own back to the slaughter. He could do anything—he would do anything. He would be the first Malaysian cosmonaut, the first Asian to touch the stars, the first fella from Johor to see the entire world gleaming at his feet.

But there was one last difficulty, which was the difficulty of it all strung together. It was 1967, we were from a kampung wedged between the jungle and the sea, our blood and languages mingled and muddy. And communist activity, the first iteration of which not long ago had blazed through the jungles, had started again.

The communists were fighting mainly across the sea in Sarawak and by the border with Thailand. Both places far from us, and yet the older people in the kampung were still a little worried. Around us the jungle bloomed, the *sound* of it—a thousand animal lives, the rattling of the wind through the trees—persistent, cloying. At night, if you looked into it, it seemed to pulse with the strange sort of light which could only exist in the darkness. Our parents had lived through the Emergency, when the communists had fought in the jungles of our peninsula. We were told that the communists were killers, ruthless, and when we asked why they killed, we were given no answer. And so we went to our brother.

By this time, he was working full-time at the mechanic's. He had had a string of girlfriends but was now single again. He had not spoken of his dream to be the first cosmonaut for a long time, but neither had he thrown away his things from childhood—his newspaper clippings, a very ugly spaceship sketch that we had made for him with a bit of charcoal, preserved with some varnish from the mechanic's. Some of the old folks in the kampung still called him *Boy-boy Yu*, remembering his running around with a piece of tinfoil, shouting the cosmonaut's name, both of us trying and failing to catch him.

All those dreams he had shelved, faced with the reality of living. And instead, something in him grew and spread. We had no name for the thing that was *different* about him; it was something that we could just sense. His passionate rants about our poverty, his talk of 'unionising' in town. Remember where we lived and when—remember Vietnam, Indonesia, the Philippines. Laos, Cambodia, Korea. Remember who we were and where and what we had come from. To the northwest was Kerala, farther north lay Kolkata. We do not even have to speak about the situation in China. It was clear that the communists in the jungles were the enemy, it was clear that our parents were afraid of them, but nothing is ever quite clear in the tropics. We were aware that we were living in the slipstream of history, even if the exact contours of that history were lost to us, and so we went to him to find out what exactly it all *meant*.

It was night when we asked him this. We were sitting on the verandah, the mosquito coil burning away in a corner, perfuming the night. The azan had just faded, the imam's lonesome voice giving way to nighthowl. A skein of lightning tore through the sky, erasing the stars, and although we waited for the accompanying roll of thunder, nothing came. Our brother was fiddling with a scrapped radio he had been trying to fix. It released a crinkle of static, then sputtered into silence. *But what do they want?*

Our brother said nothing for some time. He was sheathed in a distant, scant light in which the small, funny-funny cuts on his forearms were visible. When he finally spoke, his voice was measured, careful. *It is important to remember* . . . he paused. *What you must know is* . . . *okay, like this—the thing is* . . .

Then he stopped altogether. Beyond us, the jungle's night-time orchestra unfurled. If we concentrated very deeply, which typically was difficult for us, we could hear the distant undulation of the sea against the shore. The night air felt heavy to us, like the pelt of some animal. Our brother tipped his head back, so that he was looking at the sky. We followed his gaze. Everything felt so far away then, but also close to us, and we felt suddenly wise, as if we were privy to the mechanics of this vastness, as if something had moved in the earth beneath us. When we looked back at our brother, we noticed that his head was bent, his forehead resting on his fist. He did not want us to notice, but he was weeping.

Three nights later, we were visited by the mata.

We were the ones who awoke first. Our eyes gummy, our heads swimming. We had been woken by *something*—but what had it been? The air settled around us, we could see our brother's moonlit silhouette sleeping next to us. Then we understood what it was. Below us, in the empty belly between the stilts upon which our house was propped, we could hear something shifting about. Something larger and more dangerous than the kampung dogs. We sat upright, froze every bone and blade in our body, made our blood stop moving—so that we could listen. Voices. We reached for our brother as it reached for the door.

When we touched our brother's shoulder, his eyes flew open so that we could see immediately the gleam of them. He gestured for us to stay put, a finger to his lips, and drew himself up in a move that was both slow and urgent. He seemed to know something we did not. There was a knock at the door. A series of knocks. We heard our parents wake in their room, saw the blade of light beneath the slit in our door from the kerosene lamp that our father must have lit. We heard their confused and wary voices, heard their footsteps moving to the front door, heard the door opening, heard the voices of strange men.

Stay, our brother said, and got up himself. We could not tell, in the moonlit dark, if he was afraid. He opened the door of our room and for a moment stood bathed in the glow of the kerosene lamp outside. We saw his shadow against the wood plank wall, and the sight of it—larger than life itself, darker than any terror—calmed our hearts. Then he closed the door again and we rushed to it, putting our ears against it so that we could hear.

We did not have to trouble ourselves. In a few minutes our door was pulled open again. Our heads knocked against each other's as we sprang back. We could see them then, the mata. In their hats with the gleaming chin-straps, in their shorts. Two strange men, and a third whom we knew. It was _____; we shouted his name. The look on his face was sheepish, apologetic. He was a friend of our brother's and therefore a friend of ours. They had played together growing up, and we had all gone to each other's houses for Raya, for Chinese New Year and Deepavali. To us, the uniform did not have the effect of making _____ look imposing, as it did with the strangers. In fact, his baggy shorts made his knees look knobbly, made the mosquito bites on his shins more obvious. His head beneath his hat had taken on a funny shape. No, it didn't suit him. But what was he doing here, in our house, with these strangers? He was refusing to look at us.

Behind him our parents stood, their faces fearful. Our brother came in and stood by the wall. He folded his arms. His expression, we could see clearly now, was not afraid.

Go ahead, he said. *What do you see?*

He, too, was looking at _____.

There's nothing here, _____ said. His voice was almost pleading.

But the other two—the proper mata—had started to rummage around our room. Admittedly it did not take very long. It should have taken faster than it did, but perhaps they were working slowly to save us the embarrassment of having only a few clothes and other such trinkets.

But then they came upon the box, with all our brother's mementos to Yuri. They opened the lid and pulled everything out one by one. To see KOSMONAUT MALAYSIA YG PERTAMA (FIRST) being inspected with such seriousness made us want to laugh. As if it contained some secret message. A code that had taken years to surface.

'What is this, kosmonaut? Kosmonaut what? And this Mat Salleh, who is it?'

At least three languages were rolling around that night.

'It's Yuri Gagarin, the first man to go to space.' It must be said that our brother said this with some pride. For the first time in a long time, we saw the gleam of his youthful self.

The hammer and sickle on the cosmonaut's chest were ringed in a circle of torchlight. A deep silence fell. Again, beneath our feet, we felt the shifting of the earth.

One of the mata was holding the radio. He twisted its knobs, shook it in his hand. Nothing arose from it but a flicker of static that faded in and out of the room, melting into the night.

The other mata swung his torchlight at our brother's face. Now there was no shadow, only the light strong against him.

'We heard news of bandits crossing through the jungle near here. Moving north.'

It seemed as if everyone in the room was holding their breath. The air was so still that we could hear each noise coming in from outside, other mata in other houses, waking up other men and women and children. We could hear the geckos playing with their throats, the belly-croaking of the frogs, and beyond that, the rustle of the jungle leaning towards us. As if it was listening to us, as if it was waiting to hear what would happen next.

Our brother, who had been holding the mata's gaze, now broke off. His eyes drifted—again with that surety of movement that was both urgent and languid—towards us.

Was he shaking his head? What was that movement? What could we do?

A newspaper clipping drifted towards our feet. We looked down, recognised the English text from memory. Our brother reading it out to us, painstakingly, years and years ago.

Darkness comes instantly and nothing can be seen. The stars are well visible.

The mata brought the torchlight over to us. _____ was pleading again, saying that there was nothing to see, that it was finished. The torchlight snapped off. Moonlight again the only illumination in the room.

Over the next few weeks more strange news trickled towards us: A herd of elephants barrelling through the jungle, howling with grief; the villagers from the kampung by the sea waking up one red morning to hundreds of fish strewn on the shore; the continuing news of some violence in the north, some violence in the south. A rumour of a tiger in the trees. For the first time it became clear to us that our brother would not have the answers—in fact, he too had begun to behave very strangely, coming home at all hours of the night, twitching in his sleep like a dog dreaming of a field. The mata's visit to our kampung had changed the very air of it: a skin of suspicion had settled over us all. Warungs and kopitiams began closing on time because nobody wanted to stay out at night, not even to fight about football.

_____ had moved from his parents' house to the barracks; the kampung was divided among those who saw his participation in the visits as a betrayal and those who thought he had been doing necessary work. The town grew busier, with volunteer corps and even soldiers passing through. Most of us now stayed away from it.

Eventually, this drama became too much for us. We needed to know what was going on. So, one night, when our parents were asleep, when our brother was yet to return from wherever it was that he had begun to go, we dressed ourselves, took a kerosene lamp, and went into the jungle.

We moved only on premonition. We did not know what we were expecting to find. We wound our elbows around each other's so that we would not lose ourselves, taking turns to hold the lamp. We were afraid, but we understood that we had to be beyond fear. At the clearing, before the jungle began properly, we took a deep breath, as if we were slipping into water. Then we dove—and the very air around us changed. For a moment we were terrified beyond belief, our hearts throwing themselves around in our chests, a primal fear, but then our eyes grew used to the darkness. The rustling of the jungle swarmed in our ears, every sound so loud and clear that we could feel it reverberate within us. Trails of water ran down mossed-over tree trunks and leaves larger than our bodies. Everything was drawing breath at once. Through the canopy, glimpses of starlight. The dark earth beneath us was glittering. We continued to walk forwards, moving again only on premonition.

We did not know how long we walked for. There are places where everything exists all at once, the entirety of time and space in a single crescendo. The jungle is such a place. All sense of time we lost; there was only the earth beneath our feet, the sky above us, the trees and the air. Each other. But still we were only human, and soon we were exhausted. We found a large tree and curled up beneath it. We were not afraid anymore; we knew that we would be protected that night from all calamity. We closed our eyes and fell asleep.

When we awoke, it was still night. We realised that we were moving. Our brother was carrying us—somehow, both of us at once: one in his arms, the other slung around his back—bringing us through the jungle. The lamp was swinging from his elbow, but the light had gone out. We were moving through the darkness in equal darkness, and nothing could touch us. We were safe.

In the morning we awoke on the mat in our room. Feathery dawn light suspended in the air. Our brother's mat, next to us, was empty.

We never saw our brother again.

When Yuri Gagarin returned from space, the first people he saw were a woman and her daughter. They were working in a potato patch. He was still wearing his spacesuit. The woman crossed herself at the sight of this strange creature. Walking towards them, Gagarin removed his helmet, taking a breath of pure, earthly air. There was dirt, perhaps, on the elbows and cheeks of the mother and the child. Wind in their hair, as they watched him come towards them. *I am a friend, comrade, a friend!* The rich smell of the soil, the sustenance buried within it. The wide sky above him, that he had just come down from. He had returned. *I am a friend, comrade, a friend!*

For many months our parents did not give up hope. They went to the mata, who did nothing. They appealed to everyone we knew, but no one knew anything. Not his friends, not the men who worked with him at the mechanic's, not any of the girls who he had loved or who loved him. Not _____, whom my mother went on her knees in front of, as our cheeks throbbed in shame, all of the mata watching. And when he drew her up, bright and steaming red himself, to tell her that he knew nothing, nothing. If she slapped him. *You brought them to us in the first place*, she spat. He looked at us, and we looked at him. We remembered him as a child when we ourselves were children, going around the kampung, asking for rice. We remembered our mother taking him into our house, feeding him, sending him off with some kuih, some rice, salted fish.

It was my bad luck that I was asked to go to your house, he was saying. *If not yours then I would have been sent to anyone's—*

She pushed away from him and came over to us, dragging us by our ears away from the barracks. As we left, our backs turned, someone hurled something at us. *Komunis!* Just their voice, the violence of it. We looked back to see who it had been, but we only saw _____ there, and it had not been him. We had nothing to say, nothing to prove or disprove. We turned around and went home.

~

The months passed. In 1968, Yuri Gagarin died. He had been on a training flight when his plane plummeted through the skies, with no known cause—falling in flames to the earth. Our mother burned the box with our brother's things—aside from the radio, which we had managed to save, to erase any suspicion of a crime we were not yet sure he had committed. As the flames swallowed everything, all of us watching with our hearts also on fire, she suddenly changed her mind—put her hand in to snatch something out—but the heat was too fierce, she could not bear it, and all of it melted away, became ash, which the rain pummelled into the soil.

Afterwards, we took his radio to our room, where we fiddled with it for hours. We waded through a forest of static, hoping for a song, a snatch of narration—anything to anchor us, make us feel less alone. Then, in the thick of the night, we thought we heard the static harden, congeal, and beneath it a familiar voice, or echo of a voice. With our hearts in our throats we leant in, trying to decipher it. But it was only a moment before it disappeared, and we never heard it again.

Our lives continued. What else could we have done? We ourselves grew up, found work. Almost everyone our age flocked to the cities—to Kuala Lumpur or Johor Bahru. As the decades mounted, as the ringgit fell, one of us crossed the Causeway, to Singapore. The other stayed behind. We remember looking back, looking forwards, across that bridge at each other's skylines, the lights, remembering our brother, his face turned to the stars. Carrying his absence between us so that it stretched beyond geography.

Decades passed. We had wives now, children. We brought them to the kampung each holiday when the wilted village roused itself, came back to life with all its prodigal sons and daughters. In 1989, separately, we heard the news. The Communist Insurgency had ended; the peace agreement had been signed in Thailand. Pardons were to be given. The communists could come home. Separately, hearing this news, we felt our hearts grow large in our chests. All over the country, the communists left the jungles. They returned to their families, or news of what had happened to them returned to their families. It was too late for our parents, but we were still here, after all those years, those decades, waiting, hoping, we could still receive—

Nothing. We received nothing. No one—nothing—came back to us. Not a scrap of news, not even rumour. We did not know when exactly we stopped waiting—what month, what day, what hour. We simply continued on with our lives, left only with memory, that nation without borders.

Some years into the turn of the century, they sent a Malaysian to space. A programme borne out of an agreement with the Russians. Of course, by this time the Iron Curtain had been dissolved. The Soviet Union no longer existed. Whether he was an astronaut or cosmonaut was contested. Still, upon hearing the news, we decided that we had to be together. That we needed, on the evening of the launch, to return to the kampung, even though our parents had long left the earth, and there would be no one there to receive us. We met in the evening, and although we had not seen each other for months, it was easy for us to fall in step, to walk as one. The one of us who had returned from Singapore took in the clean sweep of the sky and breathed deep.

Together we drove back. Night had fallen fully by the time we arrived, and we went first to the town for some sustenance. Though it had been many years since we returned, it had changed little, and we stopped at a kopitiam that was soon closing. There was a television wedged in a corner, turned to the news. Soyuz TMA-11 had just been launched from Kazakhstan, and our astronaut—our cosmonaut—was on his way to space.

We watched the grainy footage of the launch, the white smoke and the blue, hot sky, and together—together—

We finished our meal and drove again, without speaking. It was not necessary to speak; there was nothing to say. First we drove past the kampung by the sea. We did not stop, only drove through the road to its left, watching the sweep of light across the water, observing the boats that were still out on the horizon, their prawn lamps shrouded by mist. Here the stars were still numerous, here we could still see everything.

When the road bent, we followed it. It became the narrow, secret road we knew. We drove past the outskirts of the kampung, past the smear of light and memory.

We were coming home.

At a certain point, some distance from the jungle, we stopped the car. We understood that this was not the way to approach. Together, on foot, we walked through the clearing, towards the crest of the jungle. An orchestra of starlight above us. *Darkness comes instantly and nothing can be seen.*

At the crest of the jungle, we stopped. This was one thing that had not been changed. After all this time, no one had come to cut it down, to fell the trees for plantations, to build roads. Perhaps in the future, perhaps soon—but not now. Now, it was still here, as it had always been, as we had always known it. The sound of it familiar to us, the *feel* of it—the hundreds of lives that surely were moving through it, that had moved through it— something that we understood.

Here we had seen our brother last, without knowing it had been the last time. How had he carried us? Two boys through all that distance? A boy himself? How had he found us? How had he known?

We were still looking into the jungle. We were not afraid.

But this time we did not enter; we simply knew that the time was not right. Not yet. We had come all this way, but to stand at the cusp was enough for now. We put our hands on the trunk of the nearest tree, felt again—for the third time in our lives—something shift in the earth beneath us. We closed our eyes. For a long time, we stood there. To a passing stranger, we must have seemed stranger still: two men, identical, their eyes closed, at the lip of the jungle. But there were no strangers, and we faced no judgement. And when we opened our eyes, together, nothing had changed. Still the earth beneath our feet, still the jungle beyond us. Still the skies above us, continuing forever. Everything we had ever known or felt, the entirety of our lives, all of time from beginning to end to beginning—existing here at once.

THE REQUEST

A man has died. The girl knows this because the news has spread through the kampung the way a snake makes its way through the lalang. She had heard it first that morning, smashing her teaspoon against her egg at the table, her parents murmuring over their coffee. They had balik kampung for the holidays, departed from their home in the city almost immediately after subuh, the sky still dark but streaked with dawn light already. She had fallen asleep again once in the cool cocoon of the car, awoken just as they broached the outskirts of the kampung. The familiar rise of the foliage, the press of the thinning jungle. Not even a jungle properly, she knew—just clusters of pokok pisang that grew this way and that, a gnarl of trees and brush.

They had done all the proper things upon their arrival at her grand-mother's house, the expected things. The girl putting her forehead to her grandmother's trembling hand. The greetings and bestowing of gifts from the city, the visiting of the neighbours and the catching up on news and gossip. She had joined her grandmother and mother in the rest of the day's prayers, her forehead to the mat, turning her head afterwards this way and that. *Syukur Alhamduillah*, her grandmother said when she had seen her again, clasping her face between her hands. *Syukur*. Her voice trailing in a request for the girl's good health.

So far, things have gone as they always had. As they have for years—as many years as the girl has been alive. But today, she is hearing these whispers that arrived that morning about the death of a man, whispers that spread after the dawn prayers. What she can glean from her parents' voices is that he was an old man, that her grandmother had known him. The other elders in the kampung had known him too. Might the dead man, the girl wonders, be an old friend of her grandmother's? If so, she should think of a way to comfort her, but even as she is thinking this they hear the door of her grand-mother's room open, the stuttered cadence of her gait against the floors.

Her parents fall silent as her grandmother enters the kitchen. Her father reaches forwards at the table to prise the lid off a new can of condensed milk for her, her mother gesturing for her to sit. Her grandmother sits next to the girl and leans forward, placing her hand against the girl's cheek. They look into the others' eyes, and the girl notices how bright her grandmother's eyes are this particular morning. She can see her reflection in them.

'Mak—' her father begins, 'about . . . about what you said to us this morning . . .'

Her grandmother turns her head. 'There is nothing more I have to say.'

The news continues to spread. The girl knows this because she hears more rumours when she walks over to the kedai runcit for a Paddle Pop, the bloom of a rainbow left behind on her tongue afterwards from the stain of the food colouring. An old man has died. He had not been living in this kampung, but he was from here. It is a pakcik standing at the kedai runcit counter who is saying this; the girl interrupts the conversation he is having with the shopkeeper, her hand outstretched with the shilling to pay.

They want him buried here, in the kubur. Where we have been burying our dead for so long.

They fall silent as she stands at the counter, switching the conversation to remark on how tall she has grown and to ask about her parents. But the girl wants to hear more, and so when she gets out of the kedai runcit, she circles it and crouches by the window behind the counter where she can still hear the voices of the men if she concentrates.

So he wants a burial? she hears the shopkeeper say. *I thought he might have wanted to be cremated—like the Hindus are, like the Chinese.* She hears the pakcik's voice rise in response; she is taken aback by the emotion that is in it—*No! They want him here, they want him to come home . . .*

The girl saw a Hindu funeral once, saw the flames leap against a white shroud. The smell of incense rising through the smoke, the cloying perfume of jasmine. *A body in there. A person. A body.* She imagines this old man, who for some reason she thinks of as her late grandfather, a man she has only seen in photographs, smiling placidly next to her grandmother, his songkok at an angle. Suddenly she does not want to hear any more. She stands up and walks away.

When she arrives home, her parents' car is no longer in the driveway. She climbs the set of wooden steps to her grandmother's house and sees a cluster of slippers. Opening the door, she sees a group of makciks whose heads rise to meet her. Her grandmother sits in the middle of them, and for a moment there is silence; she knows instinctively that she must have interrupted some talk. She remembers what she heard earlier: *So he wants a burial?* Her grandmother calls out to her, and she knows what she must do. She wipes her hands—still sticky from the ice cream—on her baju before she goes around the circle of makciks, her forehead to their hands, and when the greetings are done, her grandmother says to her: *Sayang, perhaps it is time for you to take a nap? Perhaps you should leave us for a moment—we are only old women, there is nothing that interesting going on here.*

The afternoon is long and hot, and the girl tries to go to sleep. For a long time, she is in that strange place between sleeping and waking, where she is not fully conscious but is also aware that the world is continuing to revolve around her. She can see everything, sense it—as if she is merely on the cusp of this reality. She hears voices through the plank walls but cannot understand what they are saying. In the afternoon heat she feels the bedclothes, her hair, stuck to her damp skin. And somewhere in the midst of this all, she is aware that she is dreaming.

Eventually, she does fall asleep, and when she wakes the sky is heavy with the light of the late afternoon. After a while she peels herself off the mat and makes her way into the living room. Her parents are back. She hears her mother talking on the phone in the kitchen, her voice fussy and precise. She walks out into the living room and does not see her grandmother. Perhaps she is sleeping in her room too. When she was younger she would crawl onto the mat with her, be lost to the world as they slept. Now the thought of that old man rises to her again.

She walks to the window and sees her father fiddling with the car engine. He turns back to look at her and makes a face. She makes one back and feels calmed, emerging briefly from the fog of the day. With a renewed sense of purpose she leaves the window and heads to the door, barrels down the steps and into her father's arms.

'What is it, sayang?'

She closes her eyes. She is not sure how to say what she wants to say—not sure that she even wants to say it.

'Is there something wrong?'

She unlatches herself from her father, takes a breath.

'An old man has died,' she says. She watches her father's expression, observes how there is no shock on his face, only a sort of resignation. 'I don't think he is from here, but everyone seems to know him.'

Her father does not speak for a moment, only raises his eyes briefly to the open window above them before settling them on her. He crouches down so they can speak face to face.

'Yes,' he says, 'That's true. A man has died, and he was from here.'

'Will he be burnt, like a Hindu or a Chinese?'

'Burnt?' Her father is shocked now, she can tell. 'What have you been hearing?'

She shrugged. 'I went to the kedai runcit just now only, and I heard . . .'

Her father shook his head.

'He will not be cremated, sayang. He will be buried as is usually done.'

'Who is he?'

'He was just a man. His parents were from here, his family. Just like me, like your grandmother. Like your grandfather and her parents. Like everyone who came before them.'

She presses her heel into the dirt.

'Why did he leave?'

'Why did I leave?' her father asked. 'Many people leave. It is normal to leave and come back. Dah, perhaps you should go back up—your mother told me just now she wanted you to help with something, go and find her.'

The girl understands that she is being dismissed, even if not unkindly. Her father turns back to the car, and she knows that what he has told her is not the entire truth, but there is nothing she can do.

Her mother has nothing for her to do in the kitchen. She is still on her call. And so the girl decides that she will go out and find someone to play with, perhaps one of the other children in the village. She says this to her mother who bites her lip and peels the phone off her ear for a moment. She has a city-dweller's mild distrust of the kampung, having not grown up in one herself.

'You will be back before dark, okay? And use the bicycle. And don't talk to anyone you don't know. And don't—'

'Mak . . . I know everyone here . . .'

'Wa, so smart, is it? Okay, go ahead . . . make sure you're back before dark. If you end up at someone's house get their mother to call, okay?'

'Okay.'

With that, her mother nods and the girl sets out. She takes the bicycle and makes her way down the dirt path leading off from the side of the house. This is her bicycle, and her father had tied some streamers to the handle for her the last time they had visited. Although the colour has faded from them over time, they still glitter now, pink and blue, beneath the last of the day's sun.

The girl makes her way around the kampung, calling out to the people she recognises as she passes them by. The wind is in her hair, and the faces are familiar to her after so many years. It is still quiet in the day, and she wonders how many houses the news of the old man has travelled to. Who will tell her what she needs to know? Not one of the makciks or pakciks. This is not the kind of news she can get out of any of the adults her parents' age. But then as she rides down a slight slope, parallel to a field from which a startled flock of birds now emerges, she sees yet another familiar face—a girl a couple of years older than her, a friend. This other girl is standing at the side of the path, holding a plastic bag that must have come from the kedai runcit.

The girl wheels her bicycle to a stop.

'You've come back already,' her friend says.

'Ya. You are going home now?'

'Ya. My mother needs these for dinner.' Her friend lifts the plastic bag, in which the girl can see some eggs.

'Do you want to get on my bike? I can send you home.'

The other girl clambers onto the bicycle, and together they cycle slowly towards her house so as not to hurt the eggs. The light is now turning fiery but soft—evening soaking into the sky.

'Kak,' the girl says—for her friend is a little bit older than her—'have you heard what everybody has been saying today?'

'Everybody?'

'Yes, wherever I go today I've been hearing about this old man . . .'

'Oh, the one who passed away.'

'Ya.' The girl feels a thrum in her chest. 'The one who used to live here. Do you know who he was?'

'I can tell you,' her friend says, 'But you are not allowed to say it, or to tell anyone I told you. Understand?'

'Understand.'

'He left because he was an unbeliever.'

'An unbeliever?'

'Ya. That is what my grandmother said. He was a young man when he left only. Still during British times.'

'What else?'

'I know this only.'

'That's all?'

'Ya. That's all.'

The girl drops her friend off and then cycles back home, feeling suddenly weary. The sky is a dusty blue now, and sure enough, she hears the azan for maghrib wind through the air, wrap itself around the trees, rustle through the grass, dance with the last of the light on a stream she is passing. Her mother usually does not say this prayer as she typically makes her way home from work at this time, but the girl knows that she will be praying next to her grandmother now, just as her father would have gone to the surau for this particular one.

She arrives home as the azan trickles to a close, leaning her bicycle against the wall and running up the steps. The light has been turned on already, a sizzling strip of white fluorescence, but it is still bright outside. She has obeyed her mother's instruction, to return home before it is dark. She wants to bathe before dinner, and while her mother and grandmother are closing the prayer, she rushes to the outdoor washroom, dousing herself in pail after pail of water. The water is shockingly cold, which makes it pleasant afterwards to wrap herself in her clothes that are somehow warm. She is still shivering when she returns to the house, where her mother and grandmother are puttering about in the kitchen. Her father has said he would buy nasi lemak from outside the surau for dinner, so they are only preparing the drinks—coffee for her parents and searingly hot, milky Milo for her and her grandmother.

She helps them pull out the plates and answers their questions. No, she did not go far. Yes, she met so-and-so and greeted them.

'That's all?' her mother says, placing the drinks on the table.

I heard about the unbeliever who still wants to be buried, she wanted to say. But of course she does not.

Her grandmother settles down on the chair next to her and pulls her glass of Milo towards her. The girl has seen one photograph of her grandmother as a young woman. She is wearing lipstick that is dark grey in the photograph, and her eyes are gleaming—her youth preserved on the photograph paper. She thinks now about that young woman laughing with a

26

young man. Because she has seen a picture of it once, in a school textbook. She imagines the Union Jack rising from a schoolhouse. Maybe the man was a teacher, she thinks, when he was younger—when he had lived here. A teacher like her grandmother had been. She imagines him walking through the streets she had ridden through earlier, imagines him watching the light play on the water like she herself had done, feeling the evening wind blowing his hair back, his hand raised to greet whoever passes him on his way.

Her father comes home, and they unwrap the nasi lemak, digging in with their hands. He puts the television on in the living room, but only at a low volume so that the sound of strangers murmuring is comforting without being obtrusive.

'How were things at the surau?' her mother asks as her father tears off a chunk of his chicken for her.

'Same only.' He pauses for a moment and then raises his head, looks up at all of them, then at his daughter. For a moment, it appears as if he is thinking of something. The girl watches him, her hand hovering over her rice.

'But they were talking about whether they want to bury the old man—'

The girl sweeps her eyes across the table. Her mother looks wary; her grandmother's expression has not changed, but she opens her mouth and says:

'It cannot be done. He was an unbeliever.'

'Mak . . . he was not an unbeliever. Until the very end he was a believer. He said his prayers five times a day. He has never touched pork, not a bite—'

'How can you know?'

The girl sits there, not daring to move, not daring to breathe, worried that anything she might do, any sound she might make, would betray her presence there—would break this bond that seems now to exist only between mother and son, the two at this table who knew this kampung most intimately. Just as the old man, the dead man, must have once.

The girl's mother now looks askance at her, but something in her face has changed. Her mother will not ask her to leave the table. She will let her hear everything. And in so doing, she will allow her to understand more fully the land and the history from which she comes. This is the pact they are making. There is a bond here now, between mother and daughter. An understanding that something is going to be revealed at this table that there is no turning back from. That even if this knowledge has nothing to do with her, it will change everything.

'He was not an unbeliever, Mak. I knew him. You knew him.'

'What was he doing in the jungles? You think we forced him to leave? He left us first. He allied himself with those who wished to take our God away from us.'

'Mak, that was not what he was doing. That was not what he was fighting for. He was not an unbeliever. I remember being a boy, I remember seeing him at every prayer.'

'That means nothing.'

'Mak, if it means nothing, why does it make you happy when I go to the surau for maghrib?'

'Will you ask me to let my granddaughter marry an unbeliever next?'

The girl holds her breath.

'Mak . . . that has nothing to do with anything. We are talking about this one man, this man whom we knew—whom I have prayed with, celebrated with . . .'

'How can you say it has nothing to do with anything? You unravel a thread, and the whole cloth falls to pieces.'

'Mak, his son came to the surau today.'

'His son. So he has a son.'

'He is a young man, still. Not yet married. He came to the surau and he said maghrib with us. And afterwards, he asked us—'

'I can imagine what he asked you!'

The girl swallows. Her grandmother's voice is sharp, in a way she has rarely heard, but she can hear it trembling, like her hands are now trembling, like there is a waver in her eyes, her throat.

'It is a small request, Mak. It is only for a man who has died and who wants to come home. All we have to do is spare a bit of earth. You know the time for burial is short; we have only a little time left.'

'There are certain things you cannot turn away from.'

'Mak, I do not believe this is true.'

'He betrayed us.'

'How did he betray us?'

The girl's mother reaches over and touches the girl on her shoulder. Her father's eyes follow that movement between his wife and his daughter, and for a moment his expression, too, wavers. But when he speaks, his voice is strong.

'He betrayed no one in this kampung, Mak.'

'He was working with the Chinese. He turned his back on God.'

'Just because that is what you have heard—just because that is what you have chosen to believe—does not make it true.'

'He will not be buried here. I hope that is what they decided at the surau just now.'

'It was what they decided,' the girl's father says. 'It was not my will, but it was what they decided.'

With that, he finally turns his gaze away from his mother, and in silence, aside from the hum of the light and the low rumble of laughter from the television, the meal continues.

After they have washed up, the girl expects that her mother will prepare her for bed, but instead her father asks her if she wants to go for a drive. He asks her mother if she wants to accompany them but she shakes her head, says that it is a good idea that someone stay here with the grandmother, even though she has already retired for the night.

And so the girl and her father get into the car. The radio comes on almost immediately after he switches on the engine, some silly pop song to which he turns the dial so that the volume is reduced—like the sound of the television earlier—to a mere hum. He flicks his eyes to the rearview mirror as he reverses out onto the road, the gleam of headlights thrown back briefly into the car, against the tasbih that has been looped around the stem of the mirror.

'Shall we open the windows? The air is fresh here.'

'Okay.'

He turns off the air-conditioning and pulls down the windows. A rush of wind enters the car, and the girl has to brush her hair off her face. The darkness outside is gelatinous, aside from the flare of the headlights, the occasional streetlamp. All this makes the night—where the light falls away—even more intense. Although this place is familiar to her, it seems vaguely different now, as if it were wearing another skin.

'I need to explain to you,' her father is now saying, 'what all that was about. Because one day you will attend history lessons, and you will open the history books, and you will have to be prepared that not everyone understands what has happened here the same way.'

'Okay.'

'Sayang, you are familiar with the story of Si Tanggang, kan? About that man who left his kampung and became a prince. He came back with a princess for a wife, but he would not recognise his mother; he turned his back on all he had known. And so for this betrayal, he was punished with a storm and turned into stone. Sayang, I promise you that this is not that story. One day, you might remember that you were sitting here in this car, that I was telling you this, and you might want to come to me to ask me again about what I cannot tell you now. And when you are older, I will tell you everything.

'But what you need to understand tonight is this: A man from this kampung will not be buried in this kampung. He will be turned away from us in death for fighting for us in his life. Even though his son came back and asked it of us. I am telling you this story because I do not know what else I can do to make up for a sin such as this. I am telling you this story because this is all I can do.'

The next morning, the girl hears her parents wake up next to her for subuh. It is still dark outside, although there is a faint glance of the oncoming day's light. She will be allowed to sleep for this prayer as her parents and grandmother unroll their mats. Later on, she knows, her mother will want to fry some keropok, and so she will help. She will not be allowed to touch the stove yet, the belly of hot oil, but she will look at what her mother is doing and perhaps learn from it. So that one day she will be able to do it on her own, without supervision.

The day will continue just as the days have always continued here. But she will know that something has changed, even if she cannot now understand precisely how. The girl wipes the sleep from her eyes and looks outside the window. It has begun to rain. A very faint rain that will churn the earth and make perfume out of the soil. Somewhere, she knows, a son will bury his father, and although it will not be in this very soil, it will be a burial too, in the earth. And no matter where that would be, the rain would come, and it would drench the earth, melting into the soil, becoming a part of it, and this would repeat itself—on and on, until the end of time.

RETURNING NORTH

Already he has packed all his things for his return upcountry. Through the window: a perfect slant of late-afternoon light, sharp-edged and golden. In a few minutes it will sink to the colour of honey; in an hour it will dissolve. Through the window, a strange music: the last daylight song of birds, distant children's laugher, the faraway thrum of a ball against a wall. He sees the shadows of ferns and the elephant-ear leaf plants large against the brick wall, a straggling rope of vine. In the morning, this little garden plot will be rich with the earth's damp sweetness, but he will not be here to smell it. By morning, he will be pulling into Selangor already, the train broaching the state lines sometime around dawn, having drawn him through the spine of the peninsula through the night, through the states of Johor and Melaka and Negeri Sembilan, through towns asleep beneath kingdoms of starlight, through the jungle and its midnight rustle.

He folds the last of his shirts and presses it into his suitcase. The rice-paper calendar on the wall opposite him is still stuck on the date of a few days prior: August 9, 1965. For a moment he feels heavy, forlorn, wants nothing more than to sink onto the bed, which he already made, the covers drawn tight against the mattress, the pillow plumped. But there are still things to do—he will have to sweep the room, wipe the mirror. Call on Jayakumar and Kit Ying across the street to return their pots, have his final dinner here below with Auntie Leoi and her family; he can already smell the fish crisping in oil in the wok. Then it will be Syahil who will drive him over to the railway station, and then he will be on his way to Malaya. Malaysia. On his way home.

And so he continues on with his duties. Opens the drawers beneath the mirror and retrieves his things—the Malay instruction books from which he had taught his lessons, five nights a week, to either the students from the Chinese-medium schools or the factory workers. A picture of a woman that he hesitates over before stuffing it between the pages of a book. A few ticket stubs from the cinema that he can probably throw away; already the ink has started to fade in the humidity. There are the pamphlets that would be safer to burn—there is no telling what he might run into on his journey up north—better to be safe, yes, to be sure. He gathers them and digs around for his matchbox, strikes a bead of flame, crosses to the bathroom where he drops the pamphlets into the sink, drops the match on top of them, sees them go up in flame, sees his brief reflection in the bathroom mirror above this flame, his features dancing in the firelight softening against his cheeks, the late afternoon already going heavy. Then it is gone, it is finished: all that is left is ash. He turns on the sink and spends a few minutes cleaning up, washing the ash down the drain, wiping down the enamel. Until everything is clean, new again, and all that is left is the sound of water trickling through the pipes somewhere else in the house. Already he has left the bathroom, already he is closing the door.

THE EXILES

In the city of Johor Bahru, the rain is still falling. A man is sitting by the window of his hotel room—the glass thick, sealing the room from the world completely. He can see from his seat the Causeway that stretches between the tip of the Malayan peninsula and the neighbouring country. The country down south that he had left years ago, decades and lifetimes ago, that had once been his home. Thick smears of rain and blurs of light. He had seen the news that morning—*Exiled Communist Party of Malaya leader Chin Peng's ashes returned to Malaysia*. The newspaper left a stain of ink on his fingers afterwards. He remembered then the day of his own leaving, which had occurred three decades ago from Singapore. A comrade of his had come into his newspaper office, quietly saying—*you have to leave now or you will never leave*.

And he had left. Simply walked away from everyone and everything he had known. From his family—his mother, father, sister—his friends. His one explanation was a note to his sister, left in the flat on that afternoon swollen with heat, the rooms all empty with everyone at work. *I have to go. You know what to do.* By midnight he had gone across the Causeway and into the Malaysian jungle. This was the original country of his birth, that his parents had come from, before his father had brought them down to Singapore, following the trail of labour down to the docks.

Falling asleep beneath the weight of his travel, the smell of the earth seeped into his dreams.

There is a woman many years younger than this man, who does not know him. Who at the same time that this man is remembering his leaving is remembering the night she left the man she had once thought she would marry, who refused to follow her past the border. She had not desired to leave him, but he would not follow her—what could she do? He was nostalgic, sentimental, desirous of nothing but memory. She accused him of being old-fashioned, of not having *hunger. One dollar is three ringgit, that means nothing to you, is it?* We can work there and stay here what, find somewhere in JB—*I don't want to* stay *here, how many times already I have to say—*

It had been clear then that they would never agree on this. She wanted to leave, and he wanted to stay. That night she returned to her childhood home and packed her bags. The patterned paper that lined the raw concrete floor, staunching its cold, curled at the edge. She smoothed it with a foot and watched as it curled again. The next morning she was on a bus to Singapore, seeing in the distance the blue hills of the deep country. Miles and miles of plantation. The last of Johor.

He had shared a similar childhood. He was not the son of a wealthy man. And yet he wanted to remain in that country. She had tried to convince him. *Don't like that la, you stay here, you think got future meh, here got what work to do?*

The anger on his face a brittle thing. So you think now I don't work hard?

All of that drama between them, and in the end she was only a bus ride away. But that is done now. There are larger tragedies to mourn.

In his hotel room in Johor Bahru, the man who has left the country he is now looking towards sees his blurred and lonely reflection in the window. He has a son who was not able to come with him on this trip, a son who is now in London, where the man himself has also lived for almost three decades. In the ten years prior to that, he had lived in the jungle in the country in which he now stands. That makes it four decades since he left the country he is now looking towards.

In London, his son had once asked if it was true—if he had been in the jungles, a communist fighter. He had hesitated over his answer. Those two words alone seemed inadequate to him in explaining the full extent of what he had done, what had transpired. How to describe for his son the press of the jungle around them? How to describe for him the weight of the air, which felt like the embrace of a woman? He sees himself in his mind's eye as his son must be imagining him. Young and lithe and strong, skin gleaming with youth and humidity. Possibly a gun slung around his shoulder, hidden in the shadow of the jungle. He feels ashamed of himself now—how he looks older than his years, how the skin on his hands is spotted and veined. He is dogged by the sense that he will always be a stranger upon the earth on which he now walks. But he cannot mourn too deeply. This is the life he has chosen for himself, the journey he has made.

Every second weekend the woman returns to Johor. The crowd at Customs and the Causeway on Friday evenings. The snaking queues and the thin sliver of tarmac upon which the buses come through, choked with stale lights and fatigue. Most of the time she walks across the Causeway. Singapore fades behind her as the lights of Johor become brighter and larger. But she focuses instead on the road, hearing the sound of traffic around her, the hoot of a motorcyclist or the horn of a bus that goes jangling past. Bas Pekerja in that familiar blue. The workers' transport. On her left is the water, into which the lights fall. That she loves. She pays attention to her feet to make sure that she does not take a wrong step, is not snared by traffic. The billboard above her that reads *Home of the Southern Tigers*. There is a bend in the road halfway through where they must run across a narrow corridor, veined by motorcycles rushing past. Once she was in a clot of strangers, waiting for a break in the traffic—and then the mercy of a single motorcyclist who stopped, waving them past. Evening falling thick and fast on their shoulders.

But when she steps out of the Johor immigrations, when she leaves the building and walks out into the clean sweep of a night unencumbered by high-rise buildings and breathes deep, she cannot deny the fact that something relaxes in her, something loosens. She heads over to the nearest kedai runcit and picks up a 7Days croissant or a Sunshine bun with vanilla filling. The fluorescent light is wan against her skin. And then she looks for a bus that will bring her home, hoping for a window seat so that she can look at the plantations running alongside her as they move deeper into the country, into its quiet embrace.

To be a dead man even though he is still living. That was the price he paid. That has led him to be standing here, unable to return. To have his former life stripped away from him so cleanly, to have severed even the rumour of return so completely—to become an enemy of the state, to never again see the country of his childhood. But he had known what he was fighting against, what had fuelled him: the violence that was enacted against workers, whether by baton or hunger or fear. The massacre at Batang Kali. The resettlement of half a million Malayans taken from their homes. And farther north and south—what the Americans were doing in Vietnam, what was happening in Indonesia. And across the sea, half a world away: the leftwards surge of the lower Americas. All over the earth a rising red tide. He could not have sat idly by as it unfurled.

But he would be lying if he said that there were no moments of regret. That he was not kept up at night during those years he had spent in the jungle in Malaya, before he had gone to London. Kept up by a desire for what he had left behind, for what he had confined his future to. These strictures. On certain nights he felt that the jungle would drive him mad. The way it closed upon him, the trees and the air, its secrecy. The hunger that gnawed at him, chewing into the bone. In joining the larger struggle, his life had been narrowed to this single point. That was the price he had paid.

At home on the weekends the woman does her laundry by hand. It is tedious yet calming work. She squats in the outside kitchen over a tub of dirty clothes and soapsuds glinting with moonlight, plunged up to her elbows in cold water. Around her, the whispering of the ferns and leathery, large leaves that border their house. The earth so close to her. The sky above them so free. Tangled telephone wires above the streets—once she had heard a crackle of electricity pass through.

Her sleep on these nights is always clean and deep.

When she is in Singapore, she always looks forward to returning. This homecoming. Once, she had seen him in town—they had both turned away from each other. But that didn't stop her from coming back again and again. The nights sweet with a contained wilderness. The taste of familiar cooking. The intimacy of her mother's gestures, the light touch of her hand on the woman's shoulder as she passes her by. The curl of the paper on her floor. The sound of the rain on their tin roof, as loud as a hundred armies. In leaving her country, she has made it a place to return to. She has made it an object of desire. That was something she had not foreseen.

How has it been almost thirty years? the man standing in the hotel room in Johor Bahru thinks to himself. A single bottle of beer on the table in the room, empty but the glass still riddled with condensation. 1989: the peace agreement was signed in Thailand. Relegated to the fringes again, old men and women fighting old, revolving battles in small, hot rooms. That was the end of his fight. All those years in the jungle, the foliage—the trees, the soil—consuming itself and living and dying and living again, had left him unaccustomed to an ending as sharp as this. Even when his comrades had been buried in the earth, there was always a strange sense that this was not their final goodbye. This was the nature of the tropics that played on his mind like music, that he read like language.

He walked the streets of Kuala Lumpur a free man, the city streets with all their thousand lights. But he could not return to Singapore; that road was forever closed to him. His name had been listed. Yet there were small mercies. An old comrade who knew him personally could sponsor a one-way trip for him to go to London, where he could start anew. What else could he do? His war was finished; he could not return. He elected to go.

Before he left, he made his way down the peninsula. He travelled on a bus through the deep country, through miles of gnarled jungle and disciplined plantation. The stars a kingdom above him. He made his way to the southernmost point of the country, the city of Johor Bahru. He saw his country beyond the water. Saw its new lights and new buildings. Then something shifted in him, and he knew—in a way he had not known before—that what he had done was irrevocable.

His family had come over the Causeway that evening. They spoke little of what he had done, what he had chosen to do. They ate noodles out of melamine bowls at a streetside stall. *It does taste better in Malaysia*, his father had said. Each mouthful was a blessing. And so was his mother's hand on his cheek just before they parted, saying all that she could not. A language deeper than speech.

After they left he went to the shores of Stulang Laut, from which he could see his old country. Families lined the beach, eating and laughing.

Fathers and sons stood waist deep in the water, waiting for catch. He breathed in the clarity of sea air. He bought himself some nuggets on a stick. Above him, the fronds of coconut trees swayed with the wind while a carful of youths and music drove by.

He stood only when he was ready to stand, left only when he was ready to leave. The sound of the sea was gentle on his back as he walked away.

It is six in the morning and the sky is still dark. The woman is walking across the Causeway, back to Singapore this time. She joins a silent line of walkers. And then, passing them on a bicycle, goes an old man with two young children on the seat behind him. In uniforms—heading over to Singapore for school. Holding on to each other's waists tightly so that they will not fall.

It is then that she feels anger. Rising from the earth, wedging her into place. This is what they have done. Those men and women in their boardrooms, at their chandeliered dinners. Reducing her countrymen to this. She feels hot tears in her eyes, and then she is angry at herself also, because she understands then that she will never leave—never truly leave. Cannot truly leave. That she has not left. She is more sentimental than she realised, more tethered to history, to memory—

A man behind her curses. She has stopped so abruptly that he almost walked into her. She apologises and blinks the tears out of her eyes. Continues on her way.

The old communist has returned for his mother. The wake itself had been held in Singapore, the body cremated there. But she had wanted her ashes interred in Malaysia, near the kampung where she and his father had grown up. And so he is here, in Johor Bahru, as close as he can be to his country without being in it. Tomorrow his family will come. They will make the drive up north with his mother's ashes in a jar. He has missed the rituals and the incense, the chanting and the fresh grief. He has made this journey alone. The long flight across the English Channel, then the breadth of Asia. For many years he has not returned to Southeast Asia. Travel had not been feasible. When he touched down in Kuala Lumpur, departed from the airport and felt his body wrapped in that old embrace of humidity, he felt so young he could not believe it. Then he saw his reflection in the glass of some old teksi.

He rode in nighttime silence on a bus down to Johor. Somewhere along the road the driver made the requisite stop at an R&R for the passengers to relieve themselves, to stock up on snacks. He ambled over to a nearby pondok, picked up a packet of dried squid strips. He bought that packet with his hands trembling and sat in the clammy air on the stoop in front of the bus as the driver waited for everyone else to return. Beyond them on that silent road was the jungle. He ate and watched it, was watched by it. There was a strange pulse of light within it, and he felt again the old music, heard the old songs.

The last time the woman returned to Johor, she had spoken to him. The man she had almost married. It could not be avoided—she had been picking up a few things from the kedai runcit, and it was only when she reached the counter that she saw the back of his head. He had turned around and said *hi* before he could stop himself. Behind him the pages of a rice-paper calendar fluttered in the wind of a standing fan.

For some reason they walked back together. They spoke about their lives. He was a teacher now in a local school. They took the long way home—the way they had taken when they had been together. They spoke only about small things. Later, before they parted, they hugged. She did not want to let go, but she did, and she did not look back as they walked away from each other.

That night, she did the laundry and saw the moon clear in the water. She put her finger into its reflection so that it rippled, moonlight spreading in waves across the tub. There was a buckle in the air—she could sense an oncoming storm. Tomorrow she would have to cross the Causeway again. Still there was nothing she could do. The moon reappeared in the water, staring back at her through the liquid dark.

He is waiting for them on a platform. Beneath him, the rumbling of trains. Lines of people outside; a series of moneychangers, waiting to turn dollar into ringgit. He smells baking eggs from a kuih bahulu stall. A young woman walks past him with a Sunshine roll in her hand, making her way to the automatic doors with the rest of the crowd heading to Singapore. It is here that he can be closest to home. Then he sees the young woman again— she has not gone through the doors. She is walking in the opposite direction now, her face hard and set. He watches her pass and soon forgets her. The young are always caught up in the fury of their lives. It will pass.

His phone pings, and he fumbles for it. His sister has sent a message— they are waiting to clear their passports now. He thinks of Chin Peng then, the old hero. Of his homecoming after his own years of exile. Farther north they will be scattering him into the earth of his childhood. The rain will pummel his remains into the soil.

He himself has made his own plans for death. *Burn my body*, he has told his son, *and throw my ashes into the sea*. It has been so long since he has seen his sister. He will be seeing his nieces and nephews, and they will be the new generation of his old country. One day he will bring his son. Perhaps the boy can go on his own over the border while he waits for him in Malaysia. After they bid goodbye at Immigrations, he might go back to that old beach and look at the lights across the water, as he had done all those years ago. And then, when he is ready, when he wishes to, he will turn around and head back into the night.

ONE HUNDRED PERUMALS

FOR MY FATHER

We grew up with him and we raised him and we gave birth to him and we are his mother father sister brother daughter son. He is with us always and we are with him always and we are never one without each other never separate from each other never apart. We were together altogether before we came to this country before there was such a thing as this country. When they took us onto the ships they took us together and when we were singing in the hulls we were singing together as we crossed together the Bay of Bengal and landed here. We were together when they promised us one thousand things if we left our country if we left our grandmothers and our grandfathers and our fathers and our mothers and our wives and our husbands and our sisters and our daughters and our brothers and our sons. All that they never gave us, but even in the moment of our decision we understood that the decision was made before we made it, before we ourselves were even made, and in that way the past and present and future—our ancestors ourselves our children and the children of our children's children—were all bound together forever and so will never be apart.

Our story begins in a plantation like the other hundred plantations that hollowed out the earth of this country. Its name was Kamuning. The name of our son brother cousin father was Perumal. We remember him we sat with him we sang with him in the Methodist school. We learnt our letters together, we ate together, digging into our rice with our hands. We tapped rubber together, learning the hard mottled spines of the trees that were our deliverance our hell our bread-butter our damnation. And on the football field—this we give to him and him alone, he was like nothing we had ever seen. We turn on the television today we twist the dial on the radio we ride by a mamak during the World Cup and we remember him as we watch each boy that runs across the field as we hear the details of their play. In Mexico we see him—in the hand of God we see him—in Brazil we see him—in places where the earth is just as ours here—the earth we worked and the earth we remember, roiling and rupturing and bristling with plantation and dizzy with heat and song. We remember him in the sight of every boy from favela and scrapyard from plain and mountain, whose biggest weapon is his ball and his pluck. We hear the roar of a distant crowd across an ocean thick with static at the eclipse of a goal, and we think—Perumal: in another world in another life in another incarnation, this is for you. He who hungered with us broke bread with us bathed in the river with us. Son of our sons. There is a line we all know from our Mahābhārata, and it says to us— *the others, though vanquished, have won; we, in our victory, have been defeated.* Remember this.

And the land he laboured on we all know, even though it today belongs to none of us even though we came to it in terror and were wrest from it and sent back to where we had come, so that there are some of us now in the motherland with the memory of this country that was for decades our damnation that took our blood and our tears our drink and our weeping without ever having stepped foot on its soil. And the rest of us turned over to a country whose name came after our histories that would not accept us. How can we tell you of everything that has happened except in fragments of song, except in the offering of our memory through storytelling? *Two trees—tall trees—suitable as a gallow tree.* Of how we worked until the blood in our veins was replaced by the sap of the rubber trees, whose scent we carry into and beyond the grave into lifetimes, and still we had to bow before our overseers and the Europeans before those men and women whose skin was the colour of the blood of the trees we milked.

But they could not remove from us the things that were woven into our skin that moved in the head in the heart in the blood. Our stories of men who were once like us scorned and cast aside, untouchable and decried, but who did not accept their fates. This we carried and this we sang, passed on from father to son from mother to daughter. On and on until the end of this world and the entrance into the next. And it was from this world from our world from our country and the country of our fathers mothers brothers sisters daughters sons that Perumal came. Perumal, who carried in his gestures these histories—when he danced in the temples with the grace of a woman in the skin of the goddess Valli, the huntress who is wooed by Murugan who weds Murugan, the god of war.

And we were with him moving within him as he moves within us now today yesterday forever when he joined the movement—we were in each step he took in the gun he learnt to wield in the promises he made. We were in the air the trees the river the soil that day. We were with him—we are with him—when he walked walks is walking through the plantation lines making his rounds around our homes telling us that the time for turning the cheek is over, when he walks up to the estate managers and says enough, when he descends on them all scrap and bone. And we were with him when the British decided that our Perumal, son of our sons, had become a danger to them, and they came in the heat of the night in the thick of the darkness when we were worshipping in the temples in the midst of our prayers in the cloak of our incense and perfume and smoke, as Perumal wearing the face of Valli was moving to the music of reed and wind of string and water, and he was within us folded inside us so that when the soldiers arrived he was gone.

But of course he was not gone from us is never gone from us. You think he has ever left us will ever leave us? As we continued to tap in the heat and the rain and in the humidity like a shroud he would dart in and out of the trees with his men with our men and he remembered—he has never forgotten—whose son he was. Every uncle his father and grandfather, every auntie his mother and grandmother. Asking us if we were well telling us that we would never have to worry as long as he was there as long as he is here as long as he is with us. As he is always with us. Nights he returned to us and there was feasting and there was joy and there were sweets for our children for his children, those children who are now our fathers and mothers, and so when he would leave us to go back to the fight to go into the jungles, we were never afraid. And so the war went on and the fighting went on in the jungles in the plantations in the shophouses in the dreams and waking of this country.

And still the British would not leave us alone. Still they would come to us and ask us again and again like flies like mosquitoes, asking *Perumal Perumal have you seen Perumal*. No, we could have said to them, no we have not seen Perumal because we are Perumal. Yet we said nothing and in this way in our silence we protected him. He who could smell danger in the air and know when the soldiers were coming and would say to us *continue on in your work* and take his men into the grass, who would lie so still and simply disappear. So we said nothing because he had this magic we said nothing as they threw their flyers around our homes and our trees, their flyers with the head of the son of our sons stitched onto the body of the rat. No insult of theirs could harm us because they did not know what we know. That he is here hiding in plain sight. That he was he is always with us and they did not know. And so we were not we are not we are never afraid.

But yes it is true that one day he did not return. And yes it is true that in the end his comrades surrendered or left the country, as it is true that they became the earth each other ourselves. Do you think we do not know the meaning of loss? All our lives compelled by hunger. That is the first and last song we learn to sing on this earth. So do you think that a little more hunger is enough to defeat us? But it is true that for a while we did not know what happened to Perumal—whether he was killed in the fighting killed by the British killed by one of our own. Or perhaps he left for a woman. There are those of us who believe in death and those of us who believe he lives still that he must be an old man now up on the border with Siam. We have seen him on a bus on a train walking in the streets. We have seen him having breakfast sat amidst lorry drivers in a kopitiam not far from here in a noodle shop at the other end of the peninsula. We have cooked for him and thought him a stranger in the street we have handed him a slice of chapatti at the temples with a shroud over his head we have sung to him as we held him asleep at our breasts we have washed his body with yoghurt and milk ghee and honey and draped him in white we have put him on the funeral pyre we have watched the flames devour him and we have scattered the ashes and watched the rain push them into the soil we have seen him in the middle of a crowded room and opened our mouths to call his name.

Yet despite everything he has returned to us. We cannot explain this return except to say that it began when we realised that he had never left. We know the stories we were raised with the same stories he knew—the stories of all the men we revered because they came from lines as wretched as ours the men who had to die in some spectacular way so as to shed the human, so as to become divine. And so in that way they were set apart from us. But we realised then that Perumal has never died and so is always a part of us. Son of our sons.

We realised that he was there even on the day we left the plantations, when we were sent into the cities into the flats removed from the earth we had doused with our labour, even our scant houses taken away our temples hollowed our shrines destroyed. When standing on the street looking around at this strange country he was there, hanging to the side of the road with us picking up our things that we had let fall in our fatigue. We realised this one day at the temples in the middle of a song when a woman was moving her hands like twin doves through the air and in their movement we saw Perumal. In this way he belongs to us. In every movement every breath every song we sing that he once danced to, every story that we tell that he once heard, in the trees and in the wind and in the air and in the memory of our muscles that even years removed from our labour twitch at the sight of the trees. In every twist of our mother tongue. In the eyes of our children who are his children as he is our child. We see him when we are riding past a padang and we see a chorus of boys race after a ball, see its rise in the air its shot into the net. We see him in the fire snapping beneath our flat stoves in the flour dusted against our palms as we make our chapatti and our roti, as we eat what we had once eaten ten lifetimes ago ten lifetimes later—*the others, though vanquished, have won; we, in our victory, have been defeated.* Listen now: that this is our victory as it once was his saving. We are hidden within the story whose skin we have split and turned inside out. What was once our sorrow is now a part of us so it can no longer hurt us. In his disappearance he has returned to the ancestors who birthed him who birth him who are in us always who are waiting to rise. And so we have not are never will never be afraid.

DOGHOWL

Heat dripped into the room like oil. Time moved slowly, as if we were swimming through it with heavy limbs. It was a small, hot room and outside the light was fierce, the last of the afternoon, the sky not yet on fire but molten. The humidity draped across our bodies, our clammy skin. My eyes were open, but when I felt you stir next to me, I closed them again. There was an ache in my muscles, like a slow strain of music—a long, drawn-out note.

I felt you leave the bed. I knew your schedule that evening: you were giving a speech at the recital where they would sing their songs of rice fields and Mao. There would be a humble dinner. Vegetables stir-fried with garlic. A kampung chicken boiled with herbs. Your wife would be there, the woman you had grown up with, you were children together in that mangrove-side kampung. Her face: pretty and unmemorable, her silken hair moving like a waterfall over her shoulders. Then, after your speech, she would leave for home—driven back by one of your comrades—and you would move off to one of your many meetings. There I would meet you again. It would be a long night; we always talked into the deep night so that our sleep was clean afterwards.

But before all of that, you would leave me here in this room. I knew well the sound of water in the sink, of you moving about. I would feel you come towards me, but always I kept my eyes closed, and you would do nothing—I would never know what you were doing, whether you were watching me or if you were occupied with something else. Only at the sound of the door closing behind you would I open them again.

We had found each other at such a meeting. I had no illusions of love or even its paltry, more potent twin. I was a woman from Johor Bahru, back in the country of my birth after three years down south. I was spurred by rhetoric in dusty rooms filled with books and the memory of my fisherman father, my seamstress mother. Of the first boy I had ever loved, some gangster killed by a knife to the heart.

This was Kuala Lumpur, and the year was '69. Twelve years a nation, six years after the end of the merger with our southern neighbours. I had a job at a university press; sometimes the cadence of my voice at work, my accent, was foreign to me. I needed to slough that guilt off like snakeskin. I returned to the one thing I knew. I returned to the unrest of my class.

I had been directed to the narrow door of a shophouse lot, a set of stairs cobwebbed by darkness. A single bulb spiralling fluorescence from a wire. I climbed the stairs to the sound of your voice. You were speaking in Malay, to a mixed-race crowd. Mostly Chinese but with a handful of Malays also, some Tamil representatives from a plantation just north of the city. I stepped up to the landing and turned my body, saw your face.

I had never believed in all those stories of first meetings where everything implodes. I had never felt like that in my life, had never thought it possible. But when I raised my eyes and caught yours and you faltered with your hand in the air—only for a moment, barely something to cling to before you started speaking again—something happened. Something shifted in me. Slid into place. Like I had seen you before, like I knew you already. And I knew then, even as I busied myself with finding a place in the crowd, that I would go after you. That I wouldn't care what stood in my way, whom I had to hurt. The gleam of a wedding ring on your finger, your one surrender to tradition. I saw it catch the light. I didn't care.

I am not, by nature, someone bold. It is not in my skin to go after something I want. I had been taught to put myself to the side, to hold back. The first serving of food for my brothers, following the footsteps of my mother. But

I burnt all of that after the death of that boy. I burnt all of it again at the sight of you. After the speeches, once the meeting broke, I made my way towards you. You were speaking to a group of men. I would come to know each one of them, be willing to die for them, though on that first day all of you were nameless to me. Something ringing in my head pushed away all embarrassment. I stood outside the ring of men, waiting. I was biding my time, but I was looking at you. You saw me and excused yourself, broke through the circle, came towards me. Afterwards I found out that your wife was not in the room, even though she usually came to all your speeches. You had been together for twelve years, married for not yet one. But that night she had a fever, a light fever—her body making way for us. She was a selfless woman, she told you to go ahead, give your speech. She knew that she was just one, that you were the leader of many. She was a selfless woman. I was not.

You introduced yourself to me and I to you. *I've never seen you before*, you said. I'm from Johor, I replied. I put my hand out for yours. This too was not something I usually did. But already I was being moved by something beyond me. You took my hand in yours and then let go, put that same hand to your heart. Something happened with your face—it wasn't a smile, just as I had not smiled. A shift beneath the skin. You said you had to go. *But I'll see you again?* you asked. I nodded and let you go off into the night.

I was tasked with writing pamphlets, with editing those little booklets we published. Often I was in the room with other men who had been to university, who spoke with their cigarettes punctuating the air. I was aware this was half a game to them, but they were earnest; they believed in what we were doing. Nights we would spend arguing over the placement of a comma, how to end a sentence. I liked it best when we fought between languages. I learnt from them that your father was from Guangzhou, had first come to work the tin mines. Your mother's family too were from southern China. Your parents were Cantonese, and I wanted to hear you speak to me in your mother tongue, although you had no occasion to. You were acrobatic in Malay, you eschewed dialect for Mandarin. Your English was rough but you wielded it well. You used your lack of fluency as a weapon. I watched you speak with ragged pride in front of those English-educated men, swinging your blunt cadence like an axe, raising the spirits of your admirers. Like a boxer in the ring whose grace comes from his bloodied knuckles. Whatever language you spoke with you transcended.

That one night we were exhausted, all of us spent over some arguing. A stack of newly printed pamphlets, the smell of fresh ink. The next day some students would come by and collect them. Our work was discreet. The room was small, a slant of moonlight like a knife through a narrow window. We were leaning back in our chairs, the men blowing their smoke into the still air. But when you walked in every one of them sat up straight.

You were looking straight at me, like the rest of them didn't exist. *I need help*, you were saying, quite simply. *This speech—the way it ends, like this, my heart isn't satisfied.* I can't remember what I had been doing at that moment with my hands, or my spine, or anything else. There was an ouroboros of fluorescence above us, there was a murmur in the room. Here, I said. Let me look at it for you. The rest of the men took it as a cue to leave, as if they were part of some grander choreography. Something being directed without my knowledge and yet which I recognised immediately, intimately. You handed over a piece of paper. You had ugly handwriting; no way of putting it nicely. Halting, unsure of itself. Jumping all over the page. A smear of silver pencil dust against your palm. The sound of the door closing. The two of us alone in the room.

~

You understand that I knew from the minute I saw you what I was going to do. It would be very boring to ask forgiveness—from your wife, from the movement, from God. Because I didn't feel any guilt. I am not sure what that says about me. I am not a bad person. I have done all this work—at danger to my life—for no reward. Because of this work I do not sleep enough, and whenever I hear any noise in my room, no matter how innocent—the pulse in a gecko's throat, the swing of someone else's door—my entire body constricts. All this because I believe in the work that we do. So I refuse to ask for forgiveness. I refuse to look at myself in the mirror and be sickened by the sight. I keep the knowledge of you coiled inside of me, and I return to it again and again. Night after night. Day after day, hour after hour. I can look your wife in the eye and feel nothing. I am not by nature a person who feels nothing. But any sin I would gladly commit for just an hour in your bed.

When my dead boyfriend and I had loved each other, we had been children still. I imagine that you had already begun the work when we were thinking of nothing else but whatever children think of. It was evening when I heard the news of his death. A flurry of bats flying low. The perfume of the night that they cut through with their wings. My father coming home to our seaside house, the smell of the ocean never far away from my dreams. The city of Singapore across the Straits. I think I was darning, doing some small housework. Something with my fingers. My father looked at me, his mouth open for a while before he spoke. *That boy*, he said. *Your boy*. And already I knew.

The funeral they had for him was Taoist. It went on for a few days and a few nights. I was not sure what I was supposed to wear or do; it was not my people, not my religion. But the sounds of fresh grief and the incense moved me, and I wanted nothing else but to stand beside the body. To guard it every hour of the day. To guard it every hour of the night. To not sleep until they cremated him, until his flesh turned to ash and he melted into the world. I wanted to tear the veil between the living and dead with my grief, wanted to do something that could wake him. Wanted to join him. But they wouldn't let me near him and so I watched from afar, the lights of his funeral flashing on my skin. I who had known him most deeply. I trailed at the back of the line that sent his body off to be burnt. Like a stray dog looking for scraps. And from far away on the shore I watched him go up in smoke, watched that smoke hang over the sea. And I swore to myself then that I would never again be put into such a position where I would have to wait, where I would have to depend on mercy. I would be free from all of that, from ritual and tradition. I would be unmoored and wild as I wanted. Free to come and go as I pleased. No border would ever stop me again.

There was a knock on my door, but I was not afraid. It was the special knock we had devised so that we would know each other before sight. I had been looking in the mirror. My skin was wan and oily. My hair gone to frizz at the temples. This humidity. I looked out of the window first, at the empty street below me. The light of streetlamps splashed on the walls, a sizzle of electricity in the telephone wires tangled upon each other. I closed the curtain before I opened the door.

You came in and spoke to me in the language we always spoke to each other. Neither of each other's mother tongues but one that we were familiar with. The language of this country.

Something's happened, you said. *In the morning I must leave. I'm going in.*

So you were going into the jungle, where the heart of the war was. By the border with Siam—perhaps beyond it.

You had a speech planned in Singapore, but that obviously would not be happening. You had a dinner planned with your wife at a seafood restaurant to celebrate your anniversary; that too would not be happening.

Your wife, she will be following you?

You looked at me, and for the first time since I had known you, you seemed to be unable to speak.

No, you said. *She cannot—she won't be following me.*

For a moment I tried to imagine her in the muck of the earth, cowering under a curtain left simmering after the rain. Like me she had grown up in a kampung, but I couldn't imagine her in such a situation. She had very sleek hair, small hands that she kept clasped while standing and seated. I had held them once, in passing, in greeting. Had looked into her eyes and smiled. Had already known you well then. Had already had you move within me.

She's pregnant, you said. *She'll stay here.*

You walked past me to the window without touching me.

Turn off the lights.

I didn't move.

Please.

I turned the lights off just as you pulled the curtain back an inch, the streetlamps illuminating your face for a brief second before you let it fall from your fingers.

I thought of myself in the jungle. I thought of that ascetic life, sleeping tangled in moonlight filtered through the canopy. Imagined myself eating the tough meat of elephants, bathing in the river. Away from this city, away from the sea. Would you claim me, in the jungle?

65

There is still work that needs to be done here, you said. *What you do—it's here you have to do it.*

I thought of myself in the jungle. I thought of being thought of as your woman. Thought of being away from my work, from what I did best, from what I did because I wanted to. Thought of your wife waiting year after year alone, raising your child. Never seeing you again. Left instead with the legacy of your blood.

I thought of myself in the jungle. Following you.

I walked towards you and took your hands in mine, placed them on my body. Moved you into me. Thought of that night I saw you first, your voice temporarily erased. Everything temporarily erased except the sight of you which I accepted into me. Let all of time collapse around us as we moved to the bed.

I asked you for one thing that night, to speak to me in your mother tongue. You spoke into my hair, my neck, my mouth. Against my eyelids, into my ears.

I did not know when we ended, how we ended. But the night was warm, the heat was liquid. I recall a moment of silence which you filled by asking me if I would come with you. That maybe I *could* do my work in the jungle, that perhaps—we could—that perhaps . . . . But perhaps I only imagined it, your moment of weakness. Because in the morning I woke, and I was alone. In secret I saw you last; I did not follow you. All that was left of us was a series of raised welts on my skin from the night before. I saw them in the mirror, a trail of them across my body. In a few hours they were gone, melted into the damp heat of the day.

AGAIN, THROUGH THE GLASS

The old man arrives around dusk each evening. They associate him with the ringing of bells, the rising of chants. He speaks a strain of Thai that sounds tentative, even after all the years he has been here. They are not sure where he comes from, although there are rumours. Beyond the border. Once, a young man arrived to find him. He had sat in the kopitiam looking around, swilling his teh, the tiny spoon clinking against the thick glass. I am looking for _____. No one had known of anyone by that name. When the old man arrived later, the young man had gone to speak to him. He pulled out a notebook, a tape recorder. He spoke quickly, nervously. He was vaguely handsome, wearing glasses, gesticulating wildly. The old man listened to him—listened deeply. Eventually, he shook his head. I am not the one whom you are looking for.

[...]

'_____ was born in the state of Kuantan in 1935. He was born and raised in Kampung Mimpi-Mimpi, a mangrove-side village; a descendant of fishermen who had come to Malaya from Guangzhou during the colonial period. [...] "He was always careful, even as a child. Even when he was playing, running around, laughing—there was always the sense that a part of him was not with us, as if he was watching us from the distance. Perhaps from the future, or some other time."[7]

'The formation of Malaysia in 1963 through the merger of the former British territories of Malaya, Singapore, Sabah, and Sarawak . . .'

At the beginning of his manuscript, before this opening chapter, slotted into the acknowledgements, he writes—I dedicate this work to _____'s wife, who patiently spent many of her evenings discussing him with me. This was not an easy task as she has not seen him for over fifty years now. Their son . . .

[...]

In front of a mirror, he practises. A gleam of light in the glass, a shift of shadow as she moves behind him.

'Say that again, what was that last word?'

'Perjuangan—'

'No, that's not right. My mistake. I mean, we should just move it, to the beginning—'

She comes towards him with a pencil in her teeth, drawing her hair up in her hands. He turns from the sight of her in the mirror to look her straight in the eyes.

[...]

'Traditional historiography has divided the Malayan Emergency and the Communist Insurgency, but there is scholarship that considers both periods as a singular conflict that spans over four decades[15]. The Malayan Emergency (1948–1960) has also been termed the Anti-British National Liberation War, and was fought between anti-colonial communist forces and the occupying British colonial powers and their allies [...] The Communist Insurgency (1968–1989) was fought between the Malayan Communist Party (MCP) and the Malaysian federal forces. The latter inherited the struggle of the former; the only difference in the enemy was the face of the state—'

REVIEWER COMMENTS:

- Could you please clarify the sentence I have underlined? What was the 'struggle', and what precisely is meant by 'inherited'?

- The author sometimes seems entirely too pleased with his/her poetic games. He/she would do well to prune the text of superfluous phrasing.

[...]

He looks into the old man's eyes and shifts his elbows; the formica table is greasy against his skin. He imagines that the face before him is familiar, that he has seen a younger version of it beyond the border, down south. In a man roughly his age, about thirty years or so. He imagines he recognises the voice, or a trace of another voice within that voice. That he can hear past the gravel heaped into this old man's voice by the passing of years, by drinks or cigarettes—can still find that very voice that once revolved in stuffy shophouse rooms, in union gatherings. That must have trickled through the wet air of the jungle, in the middle of a war.

[...]

'Do you think he is alive?' he had asked the wife one evening, the azan for maghrib drifting towards them from an unseen masjid, a mosquito bite swelling on his wrist. They speak in Mandarin; he can attempt a shaky Cantonese but flounders in it, despite the fact that it is his mother tongue, the language his grandmother had spoken to him when he was a child.

'Would it be very bad if a part of me wishes he wasn't?' she replied, after a while. The wind creaked through some hollow in the house. 'Imagine if he was alive, all this time—and he never came back to find us. Imagine that. Think of the reality: I was friends with all of his comrades—do you think if one of them knew, they wouldn't tell me? Do you think no one knew? Fifty years in the jungle? I think he must be dead. Ten years ago I put a photograph of his on the altar . . .'

[. . .]

A full listing of informants related to _____ can be found in Appendix C[78]. They are all pseudonymised and range from those who had known him while he was still a child in Kampung Mimpi-Mimpi to other communists, leftists, and labour organisers who either worked directly with him during his time as a union organiser in Kuala Lumpur or were part of his wider network, working in conjunction with him but never actually making more than a cursory acquaintance . . .'

[. . .]

Say that again, she says to him, but in the language you grew up in.

[. . .]

He wanted to tell the old man another strain of rumour that had surfaced—resurfaced?—in his interviews. A piece of knowledge he had not sought, but ended up wanting to find. Not the wife, who he had found, quite easily. But the rumour of another woman—

[. . .]

- *You need to decide what kind of story you are trying to tell.*

[. . .]

'_____ was born in 1935 in Kampung Mimpi-Mimpi, Kuantan. Grandson of fishermen, originally from Guangzhou. Radicalised by his acquaintance with tin miners (and former miners?). Arrived in Kuala Lumpur in 1965. Factory worker. Became a union organiser (insert timeline of associations, affiliations, etc.). Disappeared into 'the jungle' in 1970. No news afterwards. Segue from here into conclusion, then build into chapter on larger 'invisible'/'jungle' warfare in Cold War Southeast Asia. Vietnam, Brunei, Indonesia, etc.'

He spends two weeks writing his section on _____ before he remembers. He is not writing a biography. He is not writing a personal history. He is writing a narrative about how the Malayan 'jungle' imbued the Emergency and Insurgency with its own ecological grammar, how it affected the tactics and legacy of imperial warfare, situating it against the wider scholarship—

[...]

Against his better judgement, he decided to book the bus ticket to Kelantan. A shuttle that would take him to the town in Southern Thailand where the man was last seen.

He got distracted, that was all.

[...]

The first time he encountered _____ had been in a room full of history. Not the state or federal archives, of course, but a private collection— another old communist he had been in contact with, who had photocopies of old speeches, pamphlets with their faded red covers. *Our struggle*, he reads in one of the old pamphlets, *is an inherited struggle*. A single tape recording. An old man in Penang, somewhere in Ayer Itam, a little way up the hills. The recording had been digitised and now existed on a CD-ROM, a technology that was already obsolete by the time they met. His own laptop did not have a drive to play it from, but the old man had one of those dinosaurs from the 2000s, with a CPU and everything. He helped him slide the CD in, figure out how to play it from the desktop. A crackle. The sound of the wind beating through the trees. He hears, then, the voice of the man who for months he has only known through the memories of others, through text:

Tong zhi men—

[...]

During one of the visits with the wife, he hears a car pulling up outside the house. It is late afternoon, they have just eaten some char siew pau, drunk out of crumpled packets of chrysanthemum tea. The light leaden in the room, shadows drifting over the walls. A lizard scampering up the bubbled paint. She shakes her head. *Wo de sun zi er yi.*

When the door opens, he raises his head. There is a mosquito screen just behind the door so that, for a moment, the two young men look at each other from a distance, separated by green gauze. By the shift of the wind. He looks into the eyes of the grandson of the man he has for feverish months been researching, thinking he might be able to divine—to divine *what*, exactly, he does not know, but something that might have clarified for him the history he was trying to grasp, the circumstances, but all he feels now—looking into the eyes of the man in front of him—is the urge to put his pen down, his computer away. This house that he is in, with its humidity. These lives that he has stepped into. These realities. If he reaches his hand out, he would feel the air trapped in the paint on the walls, feel the

74

velvety, wizened skin of the woman who had once been the wife. He could hear the voice of the grandson. And yet—would any of that bring him back, the man who was at the heart of all their lives? Would it bring him back, the work that he is doing?

[…]

He could always tell the other story. About the wife who was left behind, in more ways than one. About the other woman. He is not sure if this latter is a figment of imagination, if she is mere rumour. No trail leads either to her or away from her. She exists—if at all—in a single pamphlet that the old man in Ayer Itam had shown him. *Our struggle is an inherited struggle.* He had stared at the line for a moment, then looked at the old man in whose house he then sat. *Who wrote this?* he asked. The old man cleared his throat, said a single phrase that would twist a knot into his years of research, set him on a hunt at the end of which he is now at, more confused than he was at the beginning. *There was another woman, you see.*

She exists for a moment in his Word document, in the body of the chapter before he resigns her to a footnote, before he decides the footnote to be too salacious for an academic text and deletes all mention of her, folding her into this sentence: _____ *'s work in Kuala Lumpur was accompanied, encouraged, and enabled by a network of others: organisers, agitators, editors, friends.*

He can only be faithful to one woman. He chooses the wife.

[…]

In Thailand, he looks at the old man in front of him. Are you _____? As if the truth would have come that easily. I am not the one you are looking for. As if that, itself, could have settled the matter—brought the story to a close.

[. . .]

'The Communist Insurgency formally ended on 2 December 1989. The MCP and the Malaysian government signed a peace accord ratifying the surrender in Hat Yai, Thailand. The weather on the morning of that day was "sultry and rain sodden"[367].'

He closes the document he has written his manuscript on. This is what he has in the end. No tricks, no slipping between myth and memory. No rumour. The weather had been recorded in a newspaper article. The date in block print at the top. The aftermath of a storm. He will thank the wife and the grandson in his acknowledgements. He will thank all the informants he has interviewed—although not by name, because so many of them will choose to remain anonymous. He will not mention the flaw in the story; he will not mention the woman who exists now only in a phrase on a pamphlet, in some vague memories. He had started this project with a single mission: to tell the truth. He will tell the truth that he knows, that he can point to. To which he can say, without doubt—*this has happened.*

Has he done what he has set out to do? What he wanted to do? He knows only that he has done all that he can. That, in the end, he must put his own desire and doubt aside.

[. . .]

She takes the pencil out of her teeth, and he watches as she scribbles away on the sheaf of paper, crossing something out, writing something new. He says something to her in his mother tongue, but of course she does not catch it, looks up at him with her head cocked in confusion.

'What?'

He shakes his head and comes towards her. She puts the pencil down. They are alone in the room, with the creaking of the ceiling fan, the liquid heat. He looks towards the window, sees the curtain is still pulled over it. There is only one necessary language left.

THE PAWANG
AND THE MINER

His mother was a princess from one of the northern kingdoms, she was a washerwoman to the Sultan, she was a prostitute from the Kinta Valley, a plain and respectable midwife. His father was a fisherman from the coast, the son of a Thai pirate, a rice farmer, an unknown entity. His names were multiple; his titles also multiple. He lived on the fringes of the jungle, an hour's walk from a set of tin mines, his house shrouded in the shadow of vegetation and the glimmering haze that arose from the earth, that hung between the trees. He could smell out gold, could smell out tin, could speak with the spirits in the heart of the earth, in the silt of the sea, in the jungle. He could transform himself into a tiger at will; he was the most beloved of God. When Kiat went to see him, it was because of a broken heart.

The miner, Kiat, was two decades and five years of age. He was only a few months out of Guangzhou; he spoke a ragged Malay, with his Cantonese perforating his speech like broken bells. *I love a woman who does not love me—I want to forget her.* The pawang looked at him.

'I don't do this sort of work,' he said.

'I can drink something,' Kiat said. 'Or I can look into a mirror, I can bring you a bird, I don't know—what do you think? What do you think I should do?'

'I can't get rid of the pain,' the pawang said. 'You have to feel it inside you. It will change you. Then you will forget. But it must happen this way.'

'I walked all this way here,' Kiat said. Hours upon hours he worked in the mines. Permanent calluses on his palms and feet.

'Was there anyone who asked you to?'

Kiat dug into his pocket, pulled out a fistful of gleaming dust. They were in the half-dark of the pawang's home. Around them, glittering things—gold thread woven into the buffalo hide of wayang kulit, moon kites, a set of prayer bells swinging from the doorframe. The perfume of incense. The pawang had to bend closer to see. A few specks of gold.

'I can pay you.'

'This is payment for my advice. I will take it.'

Kiat snatched his fist away.

The pawang grinned.

'Really,' he said. 'Really, really, I'm telling you. There's nothing I can do. But since you came all this way, why not something to eat? Why not we drink something?'

'What?'

The pawang stood, began bustling around in some corner. The clanking of pots, a new smell rising in the room, like fresh paint. He soon returned with two sloshing cups.

'Here, a drink to make you forget.'

The two men raised their cups, drank and winced. Raised their cups again, drank and winced. Beyond them in the window sat a bloated moon, a gauze of cloud around its hide.

'What was her name?'

'I told you, I want to forget!'

'This is how you'll forget.'

Kiat sighed.

'Her name is Orked.'

'A Malay name?'

'Ya, she's Malay. Why?'

'Not my problem. I don't believe in women, anyway. I had a woman once. Not worth it.'

'I agree with you. Not worth it.'

'And then, what happened? Wait—start at the beginning first. How did you meet.'

The hum of crickets through the window. Kiat swirled the moonlight around in his cup.

'I was walking around in town. Then I saw her.'

'Prostitute?'

'No! Real—she was a real . . .' He frowned, the precise language escaping him.

'Never mind. I understand. Then?'

'Then I fell in love.'

'I know that,' the pawang muttered. It was then that he realised he had offered Kiat food; it was then that he realised he had no food to offer.

'Actually I already have somebody back home.'

'Excuse me. I will come back.'

The pawang stood and made his way to the front of the house, descended the same flight of rickety steps that Kiat had climbed. He would go to the nearest house from his. Hopefully they would have something to spare—perhaps a few pieces of salted fish, a handful of rice. A fistful of lime. He was not afraid to leave Kiat alone in the house; the man already seemed fairly unsteady, was unlikely to be moved by any sort of curiosity and cause trouble.

As the pawang closed his front door, he glimpsed Kiat. In the brief moment he had taken to get to the door, to turn around, the other man had put his face in his hands. The pawang hesitated, an understanding creeping over him. There was something in that gesture that seemed familiar to him. As if he had heard of such a gesture in a folktale he might have inherited from the mother he was rumoured to have had. He closed the door behind him and looked out into the jungle. There was a strange light there. It was a persistent light that gave him the sense—the *knowledge*—that there was something in there beyond what might usually be. And of course now, more than ever, he knew this to be true. And he knew then what was going to happen next, what the man sitting in his house would come to do.

~

In the house Kiat had his eyes closed, breathing deeply. It felt like it did in those months as they crossed the South China Sea, tossed around by tropical storms, by the monsoon weather. He was lucky to be here, didn't he know? Very lucky. In China there was nothing for him. There was the girl he had left behind, whom he had grown up with and loved—still loved, in some part of him. He remembered her thin hair like air itself in his hands, her pale cheeks so easily made red by the wind or the sun. Their plan was that he come first, that he make a life here, for them. That he bring her over.

The sound of footsteps at the door. The pawang had returned. In his hands was a wooden bowl filled with white rice, not properly husked. A fistful of chilli padi scattered over it. A single slice of salted fish.

'A neighbour was generous,' he said. He sat cross-legged and placed the bowl between them.

'I'm not hungry.'

The pawang dug in himself, tasted the spice of chilli on his tongue, the sting of alcohol. His head light with the moonlight outside.

'Orked is very beautiful.'

'I have heard this story before.'

'No! She was engaged to be married.'

'I have heard this story before. Have some of the fish. Good to have something salty.'

Kiat relented, reached a hand out for a piece of fish. He crumpled it onto his tongue—pure salt. Delicious against the sting of the drink.

'Where do you come from?' the pawang asked.

'Guangzhou.'

'What did you do there?'

'I planted rice.'

'We plant rice here also.'

'Here it is always raining. The rice grows fat. It grows fast. Anyway I don't do that anymore. I'm in the mines now.'

'You can't go home.'

Kiat shook his head; the pawang inclined his. He had heard the stories of many of these men already. He learnt their various languages through their mourning for dead family, for old lovers and a country that they would no longer see. They came to him with their palms gleaming with tin residue; they came to him with a cough in their lungs. He had his advice for them. *Do not wear gold cloth in the mines. Do not wear yellow. Do you know that that is what our kings wear? Our princes? Do not say the name of the Almighty in that darkness; that is not His dwelling place. Do not name your gods. Do you know whom the mines belong to? The spirits there are as old as the earth. None of our hierarchies they recognise.* But sometimes there was little he could do. Sometimes he looked at a man and knew that he would be dead within a year, a month. Within a week.

But still he listened to their desires, their requests. Still he did what he could to fulfil them. So that even as they went into the earth, they would not go unbelieving. So that they would have with them until death some manner of faith. And he knew of the faith that remained with them, brought from over the sea, sculpted to this landscape. The shrines they put up to the local spirits, murmurs of distant names. All manner of belief. And looking at Kiat, at the calluses on his palms—the pawang imagined them gripping a pickaxe, a sickle, a gun—he knew what was to come. And so, too, what he must do.

'I fell in love,' Kiat said again.

And then—

'It wasn't because she was supposed to marry someone else.'

'What?'

'She would have left him. It wasn't because of him that she is not with me.'

'Then?'

Kiat closed his eyes. He was unsure of what he should say, unsure of why he was here. With all these prayers and gods and mystics. With these demons and spirits and ghosts. He was supposed to have all of this ransacked out of him; he was supposed to be attending to his lessons—to his Mandarin, to his plays in the village with their scripts, their slant of ideology. He looked up at the pawang, into his gleaming eyes. No—tonight he was here because of a woman, because he was only a man. Everything else could wait. The gathering of British soldiers in the highlands down the spine of the peninsula could wait; the union meeting could wait. Just for one night, he would be himself. One last night before he laced himself to the movement, before he became a part of this land in a way he would never turn back from.

For a long time he had lost his sensation, as if he was moving numb through the world. Only her skin had brought that back.

'Orked,' he said again. 'The most beautiful girl in the Kinta Valley.'

'You know, everyone says that,' said the pawang. As he said this he stood, began to putter about his things. He would do what was needed to give Kiat the necessary strength.

'I know,' Kiat said. 'But it's still true.'

ANTIPODAL POINTS

FOR ARMAND

There is a whistle in the wind and a young priest in the chapel. He is sitting before the altar, a piece of paper in his hands. The ink is smudged; the font tight, bold, compact. He had come to the chapel—to the wrestling of coloured light through the stained glass—to compose a homily but had been waylaid by a block of text. A pamphlet in blue leaf, tucked into the back of a pew. He had mistaken it for a leftover tract from last Mass.

The priest turns, looks around him. There is no one in the chapel aside from him. Aside from him and the crucifix at the altar, Christ looking downwards, his arms outstretched on the cross. Aside from the sound of water trickling into the chapel from the grotto outside, which in times of rain is lost amidst the greater orchestra of a storm. He looks back down at the pamphlet. *For the sighing of the needy now I will arise.* He knows this verse by heart. To see it here, printed by some stranger, left by perhaps another stranger, does something to him. A skip in his heart. As if there is a voice in his ear. As if someone is looking at him whose face he recognises, but he does not yet feel able to look back into.

Then he stands and crosses to the brazier at the altar, unclasps it to the perfume of incense, the flicker of flame. He folds the pamphlet into a tight, blue wedge and stuffs it inside, draws it shut. It leaves behind a smudge of fresh ink on his thumb, the smell of burning paper rising briefly before fading into the chapel, taken over by the rising weight of oncoming rain.

This rhetoric is not new to him. He knows of the recent line of Fathers in countries like his turning away from Rome. Gutiérrez, Sobrino, Segundo. The latest news he has from the churches in Latin America reached him through a Jesuit from Luzon. The Jesuit would not be returning to the Philippines anytime soon. *Martial law*, he said to the priest, who then thought of another familiar phrase, from the years of his own childhood.

Emergency. The Jesuit was telling him about the time he had spent in Peru a few years ago, before the coup. The landscape was familiar, he said. The wet heat, the fierce light at the fringes of the day before the rise of the night. The cacophony of language. The communists in the jungles. The priest looked at the Jesuit when he mentioned this, observed the movement of his hands, imagined them wrapped around a loaf of bread, a gun.

The Jesuit continued speaking, and they continued their meal. A few slivers of fried fish, burnt almost to a crisp and leavened with a heap of salt. Half a loaf of Hainanese bread that they were whittling through, almost to crumbs. *Have you been to the Philippines, Father? Before Marcos, of course. Before all of this.* The priest, who had received some training in Manila, nodded. *Not just the city, Father, but into the provinces.* The Jesuit dug around his things for a photograph, passed it to the priest. The edges of the photograph were softened, yellowed with age and travel. Padi fields whose shocking green had been muted into sepia, flattened onto the photograph paper. *I grew up here,* the Jesuit said. *Each Holy Week we would perform the pasyon. One of my earliest memories is of my uncle carrying the cross through the streets of our village. The blood was real, not just a story. I remember it on his brow, I remember the crack of the whip. It was not an empty cross.* The priest handed the Jesuit back the photograph. The fish on his plate now a heap of sharp, thin bones.

She arrives in the chapel in a rush of weather. The first service of Advent: rain on the windows when she awoke, a fading rumble of thunder. She slips into the last line of pews, late already; her head bowed apologetically, finding her place. The priest is reading from Corinthians, a verse she knows by heart. *For now we see through a glass, darkly; but then face to face: now I know in part; but then shall I know even as I am also known.* She finds her hand

90

leaping to her temples, tamping down the frizz of her hair after the damp outside. Strange reading, she thinks, with which to open the Christmas season. As he continues to read the rain grows louder, hammering down on the tin roof extension. The thin flames of candles lean to one side with the strength of the wind. She leans forward to hear him better but then he closes the Bible. Still, no matter—she knows how the rest of the chapter goes anyway. And she has not missed communion, although this time she has not come to partake but only to witness. How long it has been since she has entered a chapel. Not to eat or drink, but only to hear and see.

That evening she is back in the flat, a rented shophouse apartment. Incense from someone else's prayers coming in through the jalousie windows. Her flatmate's musician boyfriend helped tune her transistor to a station from Phnom Penh—a clash of cymbals, a low untangling of strings, and a keening voice that makes itself understood beyond language. Her flatmate wraps her hair up in a towel then crosses over to her, passes her a folded newspaper. The smell of fresh ink is sharp and familiar. She skims through the headlines—a stolen painting found in Berlin, three priests arrested in Sabah, the king of Thailand to meet with the Rolling Stones. Land seized in Kashmir, student protests in Bangladesh. *Page twenty*, her friend says. She takes a look at the newspaper, reads the headline:

We must be prepared: Indon minister. Viet peace won't end red subversion.

She looks back at her friend who is standing in front of the mirror, their eyes meeting in the reflection. The first four words of the headline verbalise the understanding that exists between both women. The silent agreement of what they have chosen to be a part of, reaffirmed by a mere gesture, the unfolding of a page.

~

The morning after the Mass, the priest does something he has not done in years—makes his way to the nearest kedai runcit for a cigarette. Dressed in a faded white shirt and shorts, he is indistinguishable from any other man in town, an ambiguity he is grateful for as he finds a quiet spot in a lorong, cups his hand around the cigarette and flicks at it with his lighter. The taste when he exhales is faintly sweet, then acrid, but most importantly—most damningly—familiar. As the rush of the world fades from him he sees a sparrow flit through the sky beyond the shophouse silhouettes and is struck by a sudden memory from yesterday—a stranger entering the chapel after the reading began, her hand leaping to her hair.

No rain this morning, but the sky is already pale and wet. She is back again at the chapel, and this time there is a tremor in her hands. She has latched on to the voice of the priest as he does the reading, sinking into it as if it were deep water. Her eyes are closed as he speaks, opening again as he finishes. She remains seated when the congregation rises for communion, simply shifting out of the way as the people sitting at her pew head towards the altar. When the Mass is over she leaves quickly, without looking back, saying nothing to anyone, disappearing into the night.

That evening she sits with her flatmate on her bed. The rain that was promised that morning has finally arrived, and their heads are bowed together over the transistor. No music, no speech, only the sound of static fading in and out, beneath the storm, into the deep hours of the night, until they fall asleep, and she awakes afterwards to the smear of ink on her cheek from the stray and unknowing movement of her hands as she lay sleeping.

~

And we think, in this Christmas season, of the birth of Christ in the stables, amidst the straw and the beasts of the field, in the arms of a mother turned away from all help; we think of his childhood as a carpenter's son. We think of his anger at the market at the temples, and the warning that he gave to the rich—Ye who have fattened yourself in the day of the slaughter, who have received your consolation. We think of his death in between two men executed as common thieves, one of which to whom he promised on the cross the kingdom of heaven, and we remember that even the tomb in which he was buried was borrowed. We remember this at his birth because the purpose of his life was his death. And we remember that the son of man came not in a chariot but entered the city on the back of a donkey. That we were told to expect him in disguise, as he hides within the suffering among us, in the day and the hour of our need.

He wakes that morning to the sight of raindrops clinging to the eaves through the window. He watched her leave the chapel yesterday and remembered something else the Jesuit had told him. He had once visited the churches in Borneo, where the Mass was still said in the mother tongue, banana hearts left at the altar. The name of the first Creator, whose spirit is in the fields, in every grain of rice, here before the Europeans arrived. That Name still said in the Mass—in the place of the Holy Father—so that He is still folded into the language of worship, hiding in plain sight.

He rises and gets ready for the day: a few house visits, another Mass that evening. The weather that day is strange, indecisive, and he feels a sense of sea in the air, the salt that must be drifting over from the Straits of Johor. They are only just near the border. He came from a line of seafaring men, grown up himself along the sea in Melaka. Not a few hours from here. He can still see that kampung though it has been years since his return. He imagines his father in the family home, the rattan chair on the verandah. The creaking wood and the howl of the wind rattling through the house during inclement weather. It has been a long time since he returned to his father's house, but he can still recall the line of driftwood hung against the living room wall, heaped with whelk, the icons of the Christ Child and Virgin. No pictures of his dead mother. It was a time long ago, after all.

As he lights the candles of the chapel, he feels the urge for a cigarette, but of course he has none left, simply lets the desire pulse away. He walks through the darkened chapel towards the altar, the call of a single, lonely bird spearing through the hardening morning. A few abandoned tracts are littered through the pews but none of the blue pamphlets that he has been seeing over the past weeks.

He had understood what it would mean for him to become a priest, what he would need to leave behind. In his training he had been told that devotion could be learnt, that it was nothing but learning. A constant discipline. Faith was the effort of cultivation—each moment it faltered was simply a chance to remake it anew. It was not like being left to fate or the whims of others. It was not like leaving your livelihood to the weather, your hunger to the temper of the sea, which for centuries had bound him and those before him, so that a part of him still would always love the brine of the seaside, the rush of waves against the shore.

She had chosen that particular parish for its proximity. It was close to the flat they were renting, which was itself not far from the border. A mere walk from the clatter of town to meet whoever it was that came across, was going across. Sitting down for a meal of satay or roti canai, innocent to the eye of an untrained observer. And the press that they used, the bookshop they frequented, those few sympathetic to them, were not far away.

And so she had chosen this parish because it was the Advent, and it had been a long time since she had entered any church, even though she knew what they always said—that even a forgotten faith would catch up to you in the end. The bell-ringing and liturgy that was the same here as anywhere else, as it would be in another country, another continent, half a world away. The cloak of incense. She had not expected that priest, with his homilies. There would have been nothing strange about them had he said them at any other time of the year. But this close to Christmas she would not have expected to hear about Peter faltering on the water . . .

Meanwhile, the boat was already some distance from the shore, battered by waves and a strong wind. / During the fourth watch of the night, Jesus came toward them, walking on the water. / When the disciples saw him walking on the water they were terrified, and they cried out in their fright, 'It is a ghost!' / But Jesus immediately spoke to them, saying, 'Have courage! It is I. Do not be afraid . . .' / Peter answered, 'Lord, if it is you, command me to come to you across the water.' / He said, 'Come!' Then Peter got out of the boat and started walking on the water toward Jesus. / But when he realised the force of the wind, he became frightened. As he began to sink, he cried out, 'Lord, save me!' / Jesus immediately reached out his hand and caught hold of him, saying, 'O you of little faith, why did you doubt?'

This time as he read she watched him, and she imagined she might have caught what no one else in the congregation had—all these other people who must have known him for years, spent the entire liturgical calendar with him, knew him by name—a name she realised, then, she did not know. She imagined that she could recognise something about him as only a stranger could, the way some things merely fade into the background of familiarity. It was as if he was reading each line not to the flock, but to himself.

~

Jesus says, Take up your cross and follow me. For what profits a man if he gains the whole world and loses his soul? Now, the hour is at hand. He sweeps his eyes around the table of twelve and wonders, because even as he understands whose will must be done, what he must do, what will happen, there is in his heart the terror of man. For he had come to earth as a man, born of a woman, to die as a man, at the hands of men—will they remember, he wonders, these twelve who sit here today—rather: these eleven—what he has asked of them? What they have been called to do?

Still, he knows it must happen. Father, if it be thy will—this is the cup that will not be removed from him.

And so he raises the loaf of bread. He breaks it in front of them, passes the pieces around, and says: This is my body, which is given for you. Eat, and this do in memory of me.

The night of his dinner with the Jesuit, they had eaten the fish and the bread until all that was left was bones and stray crumbs, had wiped the table and washed the cups and dishes, had put them away. He bid the Jesuit goodbye, for he was leaving into the night for a place he would not name. The next morning he had returned to the pantry, opened the cupboard to the sight of a whole loaf that was still warm and soft when he pulled it apart with his hands. Then he rose his eyes to a line of fish drying from the eaves, preserved with salt, the way his father had prepared when he was a child.

The last words the Jesuit had said to him before he left: *Remember the price that was paid on the cross. Remember that we are given one commandment before all others: to love thy neighbour, and as such we are not to turn away. Remember that Christ asked for deliverance in the garden, and on the cross again, but that in the end he knew what it was that must be done.*

That he said to the Father: Thy will be done. As we now repeat: On earth as it is in heaven—

She remembers being a small child, in the family church, her lips moving to the prayer that has been said by so many before her, around her; that will be said by so many after her. *Our Father, who art in heaven, hallowed be thy name; thy Kingdom come, thy will be done on earth as it is in heaven. Give us this day our daily bread . . .*

This is the prayer that she finds herself repeating in the midst of her fear and her doubt. The language of her childhood that she cannot turn away from. She remembers being a child, with the rain lashing against the windows of the chapel. December rain, a bright thunderstorm heralding the Sunset Mass, hammering on yet another tin roof extension, swilling the dirt paths outside the church. Their voices rising in a chorus, the warmth of the music. The voice of the priest, a man whose name she has long forgotten now, but who she had been reminded of when she first entered this church. A man from the past, a man from the present: young and faltering, their voices still rising over the rain.

If you remember one thing, let it not be the angels or the wise men or even the star to the north announcing his birth, but the fact that our God had his scant family turned away from every inn, that he had every door closed upon the face of his mother—

When he picks up the blue pamphlet the morning of Christmas eve, he feels that he should have known from the beginning what it would say.

~

They have packed up the flat—torn down the red curtains and packed most of their clothes and their make-up. Their jewellery and their shoes. They will not need them where they are going. The last messages have been sent, the last person from over the border met. Her flatmate wants to spend the night dancing at the nearest club with the musician boyfriend, and as she prepares herself—swiping glittery blue on her eyelids, puffing her hair up in the mirror—the music from her radio winds itself one last time through their emptying flat. The Cambodians again—and there is such joyous, desperate fever in their music that she is tempted to go with her friend—but she does not. On any other night, perhaps, but on this last night there is somewhere else she needs to be. So her flatmate leaves, and she is alone in front of the mirror. She puts her hair up, twisting it into a knot. For a long time she sits there, watches it fade. The song of a single bird dissipates with the light, soaking into the gathering dark, the last luminous line on the horizon. Then she collects herself and stands, making her way out of the flat and down the stairs, pulling the pin out of her hair as she descends so that it spirals down her shoulders as she closes the door.

She arrives late again. The candles are all lit, the congregation quiet as she slips—like on that first day—into the last line of pews. Closes her eyes and bows her head. *I will give the usual reading in a moment,* she hears the priest say. *I am sorry if I have been unorthodox these past few weeks, but I pray you will forgive me for a few more minutes.* When she opens her eyes, she sees a blue slip of paper in his hands, hears him say: *For I was an hungred, and ye gave me meat: I was thirsty, and ye gave me drink: I was a stranger, and ye took me in: naked, and ye clothed me: I was sick, and ye visited me; I was in prison and ye came unto me.* Then, putting the pamphlet away, he says:

Thus, brothers and sisters: I say unto thee—bear one another's burdens, and so fulfil the law of Christ.

She stands when it is the turn of her pew to receive the host, makes her way to the altar. She is still a stranger here and soon everyone will forget her, she will be folded into memory, become nothing more than an anecdote. *Do you remember the girl in that bright blue dress? She was here for a month and didn't speak to anyone. She wore red lipstick once, I think. Imagine that colour in a chapel!* And then she would not be remembered, fading even from gossip. As she had once faded away from the world of her childhood, as she soon will be folded into the black womb of the jungle.

She kneels at the altar in front of the sacraments. It is muscle memory that moves her through this familiar gesture. When the priest reaches her, she looks into his eyes.

Body of Christ, he says.

Body of Christ, she repeats.

MY FATHER'S COUNTRY

He watches the flag go up slowly, uncurling itself into the thick heat with the sound of the national anthem behind it, the white strips of fabric blinding in the morning sun. He watches the two students in front of him knock their hands against each other's, watches two other students ahead of them stifle their laughter. His own belly churns with his breakfast; he tastes ginger at the back of his throat from his teh halia. Then the air changes, quite suddenly, goes thick and heavy, and there is a cool whip to the wind, and there is an expectant murmur—the anthem swells, but the moment passes. Heat seeps back into the day.

This weekend he will have to go back to the plantation. It has been a month since his return and there is shopping to be done on Friday evening. He makes his list between his classes—some ghee, a new paraffin lamp. Rice and dried fish. His students swarm in and out, and the heat thickens further until they are in the full swelter of afternoon. But he makes sure they pay attention. Not out of force, not by swinging the wooden ruler against the blackboard like some of his colleagues. He is not jovial like some of the other teachers, the ones who joke and rush around full of merriment, almost students themselves. No, that does not come to him naturally. Instead his voice is quiet so that the students have to almost strain to listen. He speaks deliberately, not out of affect but because English is not his first language, because he knows it also isn't theirs. He focuses on finding words precise enough to capture their slippery history. *In 1786, the British obtained the island of Penang from the Sultanate of Kedah . . . .* This is formal language, not his own. The classroom is hot, his ankles sometimes itchy. But always there is a sense of duty in the room. A quiet that among thirty teenagers is almost impossible, magical.

In the evenings he returns to the teacher's hostel, to the flat he shares with three other men. Two of them, the sons of miners from the country, are teaching mathematics. The other, a Malay-language teacher from Kedah. Each week they gather for cigarettes and drinks and laugh into the deep night over the antics of their childhoods. Beyond them stretches a fringe of hills, limestone forests, blacker than the night itself.

He is from all the way south. A plantation estate in Johor. Every day before the sun rises he goes for a jog, when the air is still cool with the promise of the day, the morning softened by dew and the last damp of the night. It has been a long time since he performed the work of his youth. But his shoulders, his arms, are still wiry with muscle from the labour that had shaped him—the labour performed by his mother, his father, their mothers, their fathers, the fathers of those fathers, the mothers of those mothers. A line of descent going back to Tamil Nadu, a ship going across the Bay of Bengal carrying song fragments that would accompany them to the foreign country that now was his country, whose songs were now his songs. Standing in front of his class, his voice is quiet and low: *In 1957, in a field— can you all imagine it? It was midnight. Everybody wanted to be there, the place was full. They lowered the Union Jack for the last time.*

Now he closes his notebook, the ink of his ballpoint pen smudged against the flesh of his palm. He checks his pocket again, pulls out a crumpled chewing gum wrapper, two paper clips, the train ticket that will take him south.

The night before he leaves, he dreams of the river. They had bathed there, caught fish there. In between the gloom of the rubber trees, their endless rows, their mathematical precision. A disorder of silt and light. In his dream he is doing nothing. It is night, and he is sitting at the edge of the river, his ankles in the water. The air is potent; it is as if he is back already, caught in its grip. *It was at the river*, his mother had once told him, *that your father and I first met. His family was new to the plantation, moved from somewhere else. We were still young then. Still children.* He has never seen his father, who died when he was still in his mother's womb. There are no photographs, no portraits. He had once asked his mother to describe his father's face, a question whose weight he did not recognise until he was older, in love for the first time, looking into the eyes of the girl in his arms. His mother had shaken her head, pursed her lips. *You know all about your father*, she said. *What he had done, what had been done to him. But leave me his face—as I remember it from when he was living. He is already free.*

But in this dream there is a shadow between the trees across the river. His heart tightens, he feels it rising in his throat. He pushes himself up from the riverbank, squints into the darkness. He blinks—he remembers this motion very precisely—but when he opens his eyes again it is to the ceiling fan of his hostel room creaking above him.

His housemate Cheong drives him to the train station the next morning. There was a storm the previous night. When he awoke his body was cold, wrapped in the fog of the leftover rain. The elephant-ear plants outside their hostel with their broad leaves, the speckled markings on their leathery hides are slick with rainwater. Everything smelling of ripe earth.

In the car, there is soulful crooning coming from the radio and Cheong is telling him about the woman from Ipoh he is now seeing—they had met at a pasar, she was buying chrysanthemums. Cheong's engagement ring glints at him from the wheel, the car moving along with the slow traffic, the jungle hills in the distance luminescent with this recent rain. Cheong's two lovers: this woman in Ipoh and his fiancée waiting back in the mangrove-side kampung he had grown up in. When Cheong had first arrived in Ipoh, he refused to eat fish for an entire week. *But what to do,* Cheong is saying now, *I also still love her, what. Aduh, all this drama—better I run to Singapore, I tell you. Start again.*

Later he bids goodbye to Cheong, who helps him unload his luggage, tells him to get him on payphone when he returns so that he can drive him back to the hostel. *Don't go and waste your time taking teksi ah.* He arrives on the platform amidst the screech of wheels, the plumes of exhaust. Already there is grit on his lips. He licks it off. In his raffia bags he has packed tins of food, a sack of rice. He settles on a bench while he waits, pulls out the textbook that he always carries with him. He wonders what meaning he can derive from those clunky paragraphs, the amateurish illustrations that make him ache. They are almost childish in their simplicity: movements are stiff and without grace, the faces are crude. And yet there is clear effort in the rendering: the delicate, earnest colouring, catching shadow and light. Likewise, the history that he teaches is simple. Once there was this land and its tradition. And then the Portuguese came. And then the British. And then the Japanese. And then the British again. And then we were free.

It is night by the time he arrives in Johor. The hills running down the spine of the peninsula are soaked in the blue of the evening. Through the open window comes the smell of fresh air, some exhaust, the stain of lemongrass rising from the bag of one of the other passengers. When he gets off, on the platform there is a light rain, almost invisible beneath the cradle of a streetlamp's flare; he feels it on his face when he looks up. Then he heaves his things onto his shoulders and heads down the platform, walking out into the night.

~

In the morning he awakes on the floor of his house in the plantation. The walls of pink clay around him, the tight room. The sunlight is bright and hard against his skin. For a moment he is confused—does not recall how he arrived home the night previous. The things he had bought from Ipoh seem larger now that they are in the house. He stands and stretches, walks outside beneath the sun with a towel slung around his shoulders, his lungi—which he has never worn in Ipoh—slung around his hips. Almost everyone is at work already, somewhere out in the plantation lines. Including, and his heart clenches at this, his mother. But he grinds the thought down: a few more months at the school and then he will make enough to find them a small flat on the outskirts of town; he can bring her over, away from this life.

He makes his way down the laterite road, the houses around him quiet. He knows that the ingredients he has brought will be made into a feast that night. The estate has waited for his coming for a long time, knowing what he will bring for them.

But there is one person left in the estate who has not gone out today to the plantation. It is the old man, Aruvalam, toothless now, his face a series of collapsing furrows. Aruvalam, who during the war had been taken by the Japanese and brought to Burma to work on the death railway. Aruvalam, who had been thought dead but returned one day quite simply, as if it had not been years between his disappearance and reappearance, his capture and his release. Aruvalam, who now, as he passes by, calls out a name that is not his name but his father's. This stops him in his tracks, his shadow falling on the heat-baked road ahead of him. He looks at Aruvalam and Aruvalam looks at him, and then he repeats the name once more, and then once more again, thrice, as if sealing a spell.

~

Sure enough, that evening the women begin preparing the feast. The men draw around singing their songs, and the smell of fry rises, hangs over the estate, the houses. The snapping fire and the char-smoke and the children with their laughter.

His mother comes home from the plantation. He greets her, and they sit on the earth floor together. He had cut up some bittergourd and fried them so that they could have something to eat before the feast.

'How are things in Ipoh?'

'Everything is good.'

'And the boys you stay with? In the hostel?'

'We are good to each other.'

'And the students?'

He shows her the textbook, knowing that she cannot read in either Tamil or Malay or English, but her finger traces over the words, her eyes squinting at them, as though she can. He has not spoken to her of the intricacies of the history here—what it says, what it does not say.

'Your father,' she begins, but then she stops.

He takes the book away from her and closes it, and they both rise to prepare for the feast ahead.

The night grows loud and raucous, there is singing and toddy. He declines the drink, his neck already damp with the heat, with the spice of the food. The songs are long and without end, and he too dances, stepping in and out of the ring of light cast by the flame. The songs of his childhood, repeated in his youth, and now in his adulthood. No child of his will sing these songs. No child of his will have to hear this lullaby. *I boarded a ship—time eradicates. I never returned. Two trees—tall trees—suitable as a gallow tree—the trees on which we hung, on which we were hanged.* None of this. Once he and the rest of his housemates were singing the songs of their childhood into the night. All the songs that their mothers had sung to them about lovers left behind or homelands that no longer existed, the folktales in which a boy leaves his village, returns home but turns away from his mother, turns his back on his people, and so is turned to stone.

If you look out into the earth in the dark, a girl he had loved once told him, the first girl he had loved, from this plantation too—now he looks at her across the haze of the fire, sees her with a baby on her hip—*if you look out into the earth in the dark, you can hear it crying.*

Now he looks past her, into that dark, and he thinks he sees something moving in the trees, a pair of eyes, but perhaps it is only the firelight, but still he cannot help it, he cranes his head forward—

He hears his father's name behind him.

When he turns, it is Aruvalam standing there.

'Uncle.'

A shadow crosses the old man's face, then he speaks again.

'My mistake. It's you.'

'It's me.'

The old man sways, unsteady with drink. The young man takes him by his elbow and brings them to sit down, both of them cross-legged, a little ways from the gathering.

'Have you eaten, uncle?' he asks.

'I ate well,' Aruvalam replies. 'It is thanks to you.'

'How are you, uncle?'

'Listen to me,' Aruvalam says. 'There is something I need to tell you. Have you heard the story of your father? I saw him in a dream last night. Today, I thought you were him, but you are not. So I think this is a story you must hear.'

'I know all about my father, uncle. My mother does not keep secrets.'

'Not about his death or why he died.'

'What then, uncle?'

'About the time he followed the tiger.'

He pauses, looks Aruvalam straight in the eyes. Firelight dances in the dark iris that is still unobscured by the cloud of cataracts. A bright blue ring around the deep well of black.

'I do not know this story, uncle.'

'Your father was a young man, and your mother had just revealed that she was carrying you. The estate was afraid because we had heard of a tiger that had come out of the jungle, made its way to a plantation. We were receiving strange omens. Twelve dead white owls one morning. Seven days of red sky. Strange songs from the river. And then we saw the tiger itself. I remember it. I had never dreamt that it could have been so huge.'

'Where did you see it, uncle?'

'You know where already. You know it in your heart. It was by the river.'

'What did my father do?'

'He walked away from us. We were all shouting, but he was very calm. It was like he was possessed by something, but that was your father. He was a man who carried something inside him that we could not always understand. He slipped into the river. He swam across. We were screaming, shouting. Someone had run to get your mother, had run to get the women. I was on my knees also. I was begging him to come back. But he was already on the other side. And the tiger was waiting for him. He came out of the river—by then we were sure that we were witnessing the last moments of your father's life. But instead he put his hand on the back of the tiger, and they both turned and went into the trees. You know how the line of trees are so straight that you can see the other side of the world through them. But your father and the tiger disappeared quickly.'

He listens closely. All the noise of the party has disappeared, leaving only Aruvalam's voice, raspy with age and drink.

'Your mother came, and she also fell to her knees and started weeping. *Why would he do this to me,* she was saying. Her hand was on her belly. *I will never forgive this man.*

'We were all there. Hours passed. The sun fell low, and the sky turned yellow. The overseer came. He began shouting at us, he wanted to beat us. But that day we held him down, we refused his violence. Our grief for your father made us strong enough for that. For a long time we waited. A deep grief in my heart like I have never known, even deeper than the day the Japanese took me. Even the long years I was with them.

'But then he returned to us.'

He was looking keenly at Aruvalam now. The wizened muscle of his shoulders, the leathery skin. The silver scars that looped around his arms. The mess of white hair that sprang confused from his head. The beautiful, gentle eyes and once-broken nose.

'We simply looked up and saw him, standing alone across the river. Then he slipped into the river again, swam towards us. He rose on the bank and came to your mother, who was standing now. He bowed down before her, put his head to her feet. Then he stood and embraced her. That was all.'

That whole night he is itchy with fever. He dreams of the river again. He is looking into the line of trees and seeing a shadow. Its shape indistinct, its boundaries blurred and shifting, but he has a feeling that he knows already what it is.

The next morning he goes for an early wash in the river, but it is peaceful; he sees nothing strange. He arrives home to see his mother already preparing for the day.

'I will come into the plantation with you; I want to work.'

'No.'

'Amma.'

'Your work is no longer here, your work is outside.'

'Please, Amma. I want to work. I cannot just sit here.'

'No.'

He watches her light the oil in the new clay lamp he has brought. Her back is turned towards him.

'Amma, Aruvalam uncle told me about the tiger. About Appa.'

He watches her straighten, turn to face him.

'Amma, is that story true?'

For a long time she does not speak.

'It is a true story,' she finally says, quite simply. Her voice is clean, without weight. 'Three months later they came after your father. You know what happened already. He was working with the Chinese, he was working with unions. You know what they accused him of. They came to tell me this afterwards. They thought it would shame me. They thought I didn't know. As if that was not why I loved your father. They delivered me his head and thought I would scream, that I would cry, that I would die in front of them. I took it from them as if it were a holy thing. So yes, there was a tiger. Yes, your father followed him. You know this already: your father was such a man.'

He does not go into the plantation to work. Instead he cleans the house, arranges his gifts. No one is left in the estate today, even Aruvalam has gone out to work. He takes a long nap, wakes up to the heat of the afternoon rupturing against his body. For a moment he blinks into the swelter of the day, then he stands and makes his way to the river.

The sky is heavy today with the promise of rain. He walks through the lines of trees to the river, feels the crackling of air around him, the sense that he is being watched. He walks past the little wooden houses in which the owls lie sleeping. He is walking quickly, he realises. Finally he can see the river ahead of him, that break in the plantation line.

He walks towards it, looking past it to the other side. Everything is clear in the daytime. In the far distance he can see the breaks of light that promise the end of the plantation. He stands there, looking into the trees. For how long he stands there he does not know. Until the sky turns yellow, folding in upon itself. The air is electric, urgent, but no rain comes.

He dreams—he is not aware of settling down on the grass, of falling asleep— of the classroom. Dust motes hanging in the air, the students listening to him. His textbook open in his hands. He stares at the text for a long time until it blurs, until all language dissolves. Then he closes the book.

He dreams—he believes he is still dreaming—that he is awake again, that he is standing in the river, up to his waist in the water. He is looking into the trees, and there is a shadow in them, and the shadow is walking out of the trees, is becoming human, he sees the face now, his face now, sees the man in front of him crouch by the river, reach out his hand—he stretches out his own—

When he wakes he is back on the floor of his home. He can hear his mother breathing, sees the rise and fall of her silhouette. Moonlight through the open window. He closes his eyes and falls into a deep and dreamless sleep.

~

The next day he bids his mother goodbye in the formal way. He embraces her, then he falls onto his knees in front of her, puts his hands to her feet. He also goes to see Aruvalam before he leaves, thanks the old man, promises to come back soon, to see him again. He does not go to the river; he is for now finished with the river. It has spoken to him already.

Then he leaves the plantation and takes a train back north. He chooses a seat facing the back of the train so that as he moves away he can still see the plantations as they pass through, the jungles, the hills. He can still see the country they are leaving, that he will never leave behind.

TASHKENT, 1968

From the back of the theatre she watched herself move across the screen. An acid speck had appeared on the left side of it, landing in her eye during one scene so that her pupil appeared illuminated, transcendent. At times that speck seemed the largest thing on the screen, and at others—when the camera panned across the jungle, lingering on the foliage, the traps of light—it seemed invisible.

Partway through the film her attention drifted; it was just herself up there after all, and she had *lived* through the filming, all those weeks of it, had been that character—an unlucky lover, a scorned daughter, a martyr as pure as a dove—even before filming had started, when the script had been presented to her first that balmy evening in Kolkata. She remembered the watery sunlight leaking between the window's shutters. Her first winter, the air crisp. She had been born and raised in Malaya, the daughter of a Tamil plantation labourer and an unknown father. And now she was here, drawn farther west, trailing over Asia, in Tashkent, in the Soviet Union, watching herself weep in silvery light, in front of a hundred strangers.

The first evening of the festival she had stood in a hall with men and women from across Asia and Africa. She had watched the parade of nations, the Japanese actresses with their powdered faces, the East African actresses with their swan necks and headwraps. The Uzbek girls in their long, twin braids. She herself had chosen a saree, quite plain in pale grey, set off only by a modest line of pearls against her collarbones. But the charm of the outfit was its sheer, gauzy material so that she looked to be wrapped in little else but seafoam. Her closest friend that evening was not one of the multitude of Bengalis she had come with but an Indonesian actress in a kebaya; together they had spoken in halting, brittle, yet familiar Malay.

Sometime in the night they were all gathered in an outdoor square, and there had been speeches. A large torch. She was one in a press of not even hundreds—thousands—and for the first time she realised what was being done here, what she was part of. She turned her head from side to side and saw every form of dress, every colour—the length of the third world gathered here, in the middle of Asia. On her way in she had seen a poster of her film, her face with a single teardrop down a silken cheek, Cyrillic script on her collarbone. And as the fireworks began, lighting up each strange face with an eternity of light, she felt moved and rested her head on the shoulder next to her—the male lead who had acted alongside her—and breathed in deep. The smell of his cologne. The pounding in the night sky above them. She closed her eyes.

He—meaning the Director—had found her at a florist's in Muar. Her arms had been heavy with marigolds when he called out to her. She turned and saw a middle-aged man sleek in a Mao suit, with steel-rimmed glasses. The air was thick with humidity, the fragrance of the flowers sizzling against the fabric of her blouse.

Are you Indian? the man had asked, and she said yes though she knew that was debated—because on the plantation they had known that her father was an unknown entity, and she had been an oddity. Her luminous eyes were undoubtedly Tamil, but something in the planes of her face, the blunt set of her nose, made her an odd map. *Can you speak Bengali?* She shook her head. *Tamil?* She nodded. *Malay?* She nodded. A little. *You can understand English, but can you speak?* She raised her right hand, her index finger and thumb hovering next to each other, not quite touching. By the evening she had left her job at the florist's, and by the next morning she was sitting opposite him on the railway to Kuala Lumpur, from which they would take a plane to India.

She had not left behind any family. Her mother had passed away recently, and a few weeks after the wake she had asked the plantation overseer to bring her to town as a favour. Then, once she arrived in town, she simply walked away. She found a carful of men who were heading to Muar and asked if they could take her there—she had an aunt in Muar—and they said okay. Everyone was very well-behaved, almost nervous, and on the same afternoon that she had left the plantation she found herself in Muar.

There was a hint of the desert in the wind. She was in her room for the night, had washed and dressed for bed already, and was looking through the window. Those bracelets of light and the undercurrent hum that accompanies all cities and gathering places—she had not experienced this until she stepped foot in Kuala Lumpur with the Director. He had introduced her to a few friends of cultural repute, local men and women, and they took her under their wing while her papers were being drawn up, her travel documents readied. There was a party one evening, a rambunctious affair on a quiet street. A bungalow bordered by bougainvillea, an older woman using a paintbrush to swipe a streak of red across her lips.

The air from the moment she left the plantation was different—it was still balmy, tropical, but no longer was it weighed down with the particular crackle, the static heat of the plantation. In the bungalow the air had been light and perfumed by the flowers outside. There was no cacophony of owls, only the occasional streak and shriek of a bat. Then in Kolkata the air had been clotted with dust, dyed by the red watery winter sun seeping through her window. And now here she was, so far away—close to the heart of the continent. In Soviet country. For so many years her face had only been known to her by accident. A glimpse in the river, in a temple mirror, a shadow in someone's eye. And in the past year it had been suddenly everywhere, large, looming over strangers, a face that was faintly sorrowful, like that of a saint. She was not considered charming, like some of the other actresses who could convey a luminous and light-hearted sort of character with a tilt of the lips. But the Director had recognised something in her in Muar. The arrowhead of accident that had landed her here.

The film that she was starring in—that was being screened here, in Tashkent—had a very simple plot. The Director was firm about doing away with *flourish* and *gimmick*. He was drawn to mundanity with the mystical assurance of an ascetic. It was her life as a girl in three stages. As a child growing up in a rural village, who yearned for nothing more than to leave and enter the wide world. And then her life as a young woman in the city, where she found work, married, had children. And then she would return to the village in which she had been raised in a brief final scene, as an old woman. The scenes in the city were all harried, disjointed, so that to return to the long, single shot of an old woman standing at a kitchen window, looking out into a field of lalang with a snake of wind running through, was a relief.

Of course there were two other actors playing the same character: a child and an old lady. The first was too young for travel, the second too old. So she was here in Tashkent as the only representative of the character they shared. In that sense she was unmoored from the larger history of the film's internal universe. While Bengali flowed out of the child actress' mouth like a braid of flowers, she was only then just starting to pick up the language. But her halting speech was actually prized by the Director.

A tentative and vulnerable performance, conveyed almost entirely by the theatre of the eyes. Or so some critic had written anyway. On certain mornings, in her Kolkata flat, she would look into the mirror and speak to herself in Tamil, sing quietly to herself in her little Malay. Those two languages of her childhood receding to privacy, curling into a secret thing, a code.

And now in Tashkent, a hundred languages. The edge of Asia held up, the edge of Africa. Time and geography crumpled as if in a fist.

This was to be the new century. She had been born after the world wars, the butchered half-decade. *The rise of the third world*, the Director had labelled the zeitgeist. His fist raised in a hot, crowded room urgent with the scent of electricity. A hint of rain in the distance and a crackle in the naked wires hanging overhead. Red on the walls, red in speech. India was barely a decade independent. Malaya itself had only just lowered the Union Jack.

The sun has set on the British empire, it will set on the West, it will rise in the East! The swell of Asia was only a matter of time. The cinema of the proletariat that would capture the moment was now unfurling across the south of the world. This was the Bengali she was learning, but she was no stranger to the doctrine even without that scaffolding of vocabulary. This was the type of history that transcended the rigidity of language. Rhetoric transcending grammar and gimmick. *What are you thinking about?* the Director had said to her in a space between scenes. She had been staring out of a window, at the traffic in the streets, the grey in the air. She looked up at him. *Nothing*, she replied. There was grit on her wrist and the camera in her face, tracking each movement, each slip of the wind. She wanted to keep something for herself, even if it was only a flickering thought or a feeling. *Nothing*, she said again.

~

The next morning the first screening she attended was of a film from a nation known as Algeria. The mother language had been upended by French, and then the various hierarchies of translations. She was sitting next to the actor who had led alongside her, and he asked if she needed help understanding, but she shook her head. It had become a sort of game to her—to try and divine everything only from the tone of voice, from action, from facial expression.

For dinner they went into the city. Now she was in the heart of all that light and colour. The narrow, winding streets with the high walls penning them in. The archways. The bread that they broke was round, a hollowing in the middle. Even now, though she had been away from the plantation for many months, she still liked to hold food in her mouth, to feel the shock of taste and texture, a pleasure that deepened. She was in the heart of all this activity but only as an observer; she could melt into it without participating. Not in the speeches or the singing as the table erupted into festivity. The leading man held his hand out, asking her to dance with him, but she declined, shaking her head and smiling. Unfazed, used to this from her, he reached for another woman and together they spun to the sound of drums and cymbals.

She tore off another piece of bread. *You must learn to live in this world,* the Director said, a glass raised to his lips. She nodded and thought, *I am here, here I am, isn't that enough?* She gazed at a spindle of light on the foot of her leading man's shoe. The song ended. She placed a piece of bread on her tongue.

In the plantation there had been a folk song: *I boarded the ship—my time eradicates—the ship I boarded never returned.* The litany of grief torn from the first of the workers who had come over from the mother country, passed down from father to daughter, mother to son. Even though she had seen no sea until her journey to Kolkata, the blue sweep of the Bay of Bengal. The same sea her maternal ancestry had crossed. As a child she had sung songs to herself. Was she a child of a Mat Salleh? A Malay? The overseer had started looking at her, and she had made herself bold enough to ask for the favour, the trip to town. Blinking slowly, hating herself, hating the scorch of his eyes on her neck, but willing to bear with it for escape. How much did any of that history matter? She was here now, in a foreign country, and what was on her mind were the old songs. *Tall—grow—tree—it is a suitable gallow*. The stink of toddy and the frustration of desire with no country to land on. She was watching herself move onscreen, watching that speck in her eye. In the row in front of her was the Afghan delegation, and she watched one of them bend low to another, the light of the screen contouring his lips. Something in Japanese was murmured somewhere else.

She watched herself place her hand on the trunk of a tree, and then it rose to her, a memory—a story she had heard. About a man named Nathan, a series of strikes. The year 1941.

It was a story she had not known until she had met the Director. The story of when the workers had laid down their tools and said, *Enough. We want an end to the molestation of our womenfolk. We want to be granted these: the freedom of speech and of assembly. We want the permission to remain mounted on our bicycles in front of European managers and their Asian staff.* All of this had occurred a little before her birth. She had not known until she was in Kolkata, sitting at another gathering of the Director's, the hand of some old woman motherly on her scalp. *This is your history*, the Director said, showing her a sheaf of papers—newspaper articles, written reports.

There were no photographs, but she did not need them: she could imagine very well what it must have been like. The thin trees with their stippled trunks like a multitude of eyes, the sap weeping from them. She remembered her mother lifting the threadbare edge of her saree to her forehead, wiping off the sweat, remembered that very sweat leaking into her own eyes until she blinked it out. Remembered the hunger that she had made a companion, something to talk to, just so that she could bear with it. Remembered the eyes of the overseer tracing her face, slipping down her neck.

You must understand what we are doing, what we are all doing. What we are all working towards. The consciousness of the proletariat—

She felt, then, that although she did not know of this particular story, she must have known something like it. Must have heard something like it, trickled towards her through rumour or folksong. That knowledge did something to her, sent a ripple through her heart. That there were many— are many—like her, all through the peninsula of the country she had left. That they had once stilled a plantation with their demands, with their voice. A voice that she understood—as she raised her eyes to meet the Director's—that he could not provide her with. A voice that had to come from her, and all that she had come from.

Later on, when everyone had migrated to some other room, she came back, picked up the papers. She could not read any of it, but she knew that she had been irrevocably changed. She thought then of the life that she had once led, in the midst of the plantation lines. The life she had imagined she had left but which she realised now—holding on to the words that she could not read—would always be within her, for the rest of her life and all the lives that she would live, in all the worlds after.

Later, applause filled the theatre. She grabbed the leading man's hand, leant over. *Do you see*, she asked in her halting Bengali, *that speck on the screen?* He shook his head. *What speck? It was perfect—everything—everything was brilliant—all perfect, perfect. And you, my dove—all of us together, here in this room, in this city, on this earth—perfect.*

What did the city look like from afar? She imagined a glow in the desert, a circle of light that expands, rises. That encases the globe.

She was brought back to the train on which she had left Johor, brought back to that blue evening, a colour as tender as a heartbeat. She was brought back to the dark jungle, the sight of it rushing past, the call of birds in the distance, the silhouette of hills against the sky. What had she felt then, as she was leaving? With the full knowledge that her life was about to be changed forever? *You must learn to live in this world.*

There—the sharp stink of rubber that still pierced her dreams. When she closed her eyes she could see the river, that luminous thread in which they had sometimes bathed and washed. When she opened her eyes she could see it still. Her shoulders still wiry from that labour, her bones pushing against the skin. She said something in one language, then another. This was her life. Outside people were gathered, in joy or grief or anger. In mourning or in celebration. And she understood now. There was always—and will always be—work to be done.

ATLANTIC CITY

I tell you something my father tell me long time back. Once you got that feeling macam you win something—maybe gambling, maybe got some amoi, whatever also can—whatever it is, once you got that feeling you win something, that is when actually you better don't be so happy. Why? Because if win now surely means you next time must lose.

My father. Last time I saw that fella I also was small only. Think maybe nine or ten years. Okay la, not sure why pretending macam I tak tau—I was nine year old. I remember the last time I see him. Still early, morning. My mother go to see neighbour and he standing there outside the door. I still remember something—something . . . something tak betul la, about his face. No, that's not correct—wait. Not say there was something *wrong*, tapi there was something not—not. Aiya. Got something the Malays say that I cannot remember liao, in English also I cannot—something macam. Okay, try one more time—long time my father was looking out the window, then when he see me looking at him his face change and it feel like last time when my mother always tell me to take care my younger sister when she is still small, still a baby, tapi she never actually grow up, kan, to become more than just baby only, but there was something about my father face that day like—macam—macam—something got change la, okay? You see la actually this one your fault. Call yourself a Cantonese but Cantonese also you tak pandai. What? Mou ah. I don't know how to say in Mandarin also. Your own mother tongue. Never mind. Your Hokkien how? Pun tak pandai? *Wah.* You really one jiak kentang.

You want me to start at the beginning? But the beginning you know already la, kan? What year la, who la, when and why—all that you pandai, what. That one is your job. Tapi okay la, want to start from the beginning then start from the beginning. Must I tell you the date, the tahun all—no ah, you know already, kan? Memang la. That one is your job. So, the beginning—the morning that—no? Earlier? When they moved us? Siapa? The British? Okay. Not that I remember so much also. Eh, you not Hakka hor? Hakka pun tak fah—okay, never mind. Don't disturb you liao. Because I just remember only, have one song that they all got sing when they want to warn the Min Yuen got the British nearby. Hakka song. Aiya you see la, now I have to think how to say in English. Something about bamboo and wind, about how we must makan this ikan masin and nasi day in day out, bloody bosan I tell you.

Anyway.

I still small, what, when the British tell us to move from there. Dulu we stay at one kampung there call Kampung Serai. Cannot remember much also, just that I got one small dog there only. I remember his name. *Wei Wei*. No meaning one, this name. Just a sound only. Wei Wei. One anjing kampung, smart fella, can catch fish can chase monyet all. Don't know what happen to him also when we go away tapi I am sure he know what to do—smart fella, want to take him the British also don't let us take. Where? Oh, Pahang lor. We still now in Pahang what, hor? Until I die also I tell you I won't go anywhere one. Try one thousand times to leave this place always find my way back only. Fated. That's what the Malays say. This is my nasib. Want to run one thousand times also cannot run. My father use to say also. Maybe I start there la hor. Really from the beginning.

My father and my mother. My father's father came from Guangdong, went straight to Ipoh. He kerja in the mines there. You know la hor this history, how many of us come, work in the mines all. My mother's side here for many years already. Think she had one great-grandmother from Hong Kong or what, tapi otherwise they from Penang one. Fishermen. So they meet like that lor, up north. No, where got gambar. You tell me la last time what camera they can find? You think camera grow like pineapple, is it?

Can find anywhere one, is it? Okay la never mind—don't disturb you already. I know this story is about them actually.

Not sure also how they meet. Tapi they not macam my friends' parents, all. You know la sometimes when people married long time, feel like they tak boleh tahan each other liao. My father and mother, not like that. Last time kasih I malu, tau? See them there one kind, sweet sweet—I tak boleh tahan, I tell you. Last time la. I also don't know what was going to happen what, hor? Tapi if you want me to tell you honestly see how the two of them behave around each other then me myself marry two women only for both times to cabut—wa. Sometimes when you lucky only then you lucky. Ada nasib.

Tapi actually their parents don't like each other one. My mother's father say to her, *You want to marry this kind of fella, anything also don't know how to do? Drive one lorry only up and down?* My father's mother say to him, *You want to marry a fishmonger's daughter? Every day eat fish?* So how? How else lor. Both run away from home, pakai my father's motor—ride all the way down, end up in Pahang. You ever ride motor? Don't know how, hor? See your face also I know. Never mind, you see outside there—my daughter's motor—later when she come home I ask her to bring you. Maybe then you will understand. All the way down. How? End up here lor. Bloody Pahang.

Then how? Then got me lor. By that time they already settle down first in Kampung Serai. My father still driving lorry, my mother doing this and that. Fishmonger's daughter—cleaning the fish for this uncle also can, washing clothes also can. I mean at the end of the day, both their parents not wrong la, but I tell you—this one I can promise you—they were happy. You think is a bit, a bit funny la right? When I born it was perang that time, those Japanese dog. Then after that British mosquito. Tapi what I remember is that they were happy when they were together, whenever I see them together.

I remember when my that baby sister pass away—okay la then they were not happy, but I remember one night, seeing my father holding my mother, singing some old children's song to her. They were like that one. Maybe it's because they don't see each other all the time. I don't know also. During the war my father was sometimes here sometimes not here. Sometimes he was inside. Tau kan, what I trying to say? Masuk hutan. My mother have to stay with me lor. Still I can remember her planting her ubi kayu la, keladi la, nangka la, with the rest of the women. Learning the songs. Then the Japanese leave and the British balik, and then we are no more at Kampung Serai.

Sorry. You show me that piece of paper also no use la, boy. You think the British got show us this kind of map when they bring us there? How I know where is this kampung baru they bring us to? So many one hundred thousand kampung like that all over the place that time. You show me one map, how to see when from so up high? Think la, boy—we all move here move there, go up go down, how can you show me one map and ask me to point and say *there, this one.* You think got so easy one? This kind of story, everybody also headless chicken, also lost I tell you. Tapi if you want me to drive, no problem. Tomorrow also I can take you. That I remember because every time I still go back. To pai pai at the grave.

Actually, if I think now. Also I not sure why my father tell me that— that when you win, also you must know you are going to lose. Even before that baby sister he say this. Tapi he himself one time also never act like got lose. You know what he say to me when I complain about the kampung baru, when I scared when he masuk hutan . . . you see your mother there, he say, and you know I am somewhere around. Then for what you want to be scared? I see your mother there, or I don't see her also I know she is there, somewhere in this world—and I promise you, I am not scared of anything.

You see my two hands like this? He put like this, like want to box. Nothing in this world ever to be scared.

Boy, can I tell you the truth anot. I don't want to tell that part of the story yet.

Okay, can. We talk about what happened few years back only. That lawyer from KL and that trip to that London. I got one suit, necktie everything. My daughter was the one who help me choose. Aiya, you know also what happen in the end la. All the big wayang there, their mahkamah, their judge. Say they don't want to hear the case, all. That too much time pass already. You tell me now, what time? No such thing as time pass. Because what happen there, every single day it is still following me.

I tell you what I want. What I want to say to them if my English is better. Actually to you I feel like I mau cakap Cantonese also, tapi you tak pandai, hor? So I will say it like this. Harap lu faham. You and your notebook. I hope you write down there and tell the whole world. I want them to say sorry. Simple as that. I want to see that bloody judge and his orang putih face, and I want him to say—what happen that day, it is wrong. Because I tell you now: even if it is true, even if my father was Min Yuen, Ma Gong, bandit, commie—whatever it is. Whatever it is. One thousand years, one thousand sorry also I will never forgive. I will never ever forgive. Even if what happen to him is his nasib. I want the judge to say to me: we are sorry and it is wrong and I want to say to him back—you think that is enough? Forever also never enough.

Okay. Let me tell you now. Go back to the beginning. That morning, kan? My father standing there and when he saw me he open his mouth, macam mau cakap. Tapi I will until now until I die also never know what he want to say because then my mother came back home and her face I can remember one-hundred-and-one percent. She say this to my father: _____.

Sorry, forgot you tak pandai. I say one more time in English. She say, *You need to run. Now.* That's what I remember.

But you know la, by that time. Too late. That's why we are sitting here together, that's why I got this story to tell you.

By that time, the British reach already. I remember I can hear all the dogs barking, people start screaming already. And I remember my father walking to me—I still don't know what is it he want to say—but then the door they kick down macam, macam—

No. I can continue.

What you think happen next? You pun tau, kan? Must take five men to pull my father out. Two men to take me from my mother, three men to stop my mother. Ten orang putih to handle three of us kampung dogs. I can still remember how that one fella holding me smell like. And I really feel like one dog because I can smell that he is scared. Must be younger than you now. Tapi by now hope he mati. That he is gone. No. I hope he live long long and every single day he remember also. I can tell he scared and he let go a little bit so I bite him on the wrist, hard macam I really am one dog like that and he screamed like one—like one—like one don't know what and he push me like this, slam me against the wall. Until got blood there. See, where I touch, here? I still remember. Can still feel from so long ago. Even though no scar nothing. And of course I start crying and my mother shouting, shouting until now I still can hear, so pain to hear her voice until—just like that lor, sei lo. Sound like one whip. Like one horse somewhere kena pukul. And then I had no more father.

~

Tapi you know also la, the end is not that simple. They had their kayu, they whack ten, twenty times. Until the body is all like—all like. You saw also the gambar, what they do to the others. How they potong their heads. Like the Japanese. Hold them up for gambar, smiling smiling. But you tau la, memang tau. This is your job to know.

Actually, quite simple also this story. Take so long to prepare tapi in the end use so few words only.

Got this one time my father take us with him when he drive up. Actually that time he was delivering rice I think. So go all the way into Thailand. Until now I never see my grandparents—but of course la, now they long time no more also. But we got pass by before Ipoh. Actually not suppose to one la, that lorry is the work lorry one, cannot just use anyhow. But one time my father bring us and drop us at Ipoh. We drive when it's dark, when it's night, and that feeling—when everything is quiet, everything tidur and you alone there on the road. I think that's how it was also la, hor? My father and mother. When they leave Penang, when they leave Ipoh. To come down here. You ask me to explain in Malay Mandarin Cantonese Hokkien also I cannot.

Sorry. Don't know also why I am telling you this story. So many things I tell you already—big thing, all this sejarah-sejarah that you come and find. Then now talking this one story, from nowhere. But this is something that I remember. Something that is good. Anyway, sit la there, my mother sleeping on one side and the other side my father driving. And outside I can see the limestones—the first time I see the limestones, outside his window.

And got the—the—what is it in English? Kabut. All over the limestones. Like clouds. And my father saw me there looking-looking, sitting there quiet-quiet only, and he say, *One day we go to Penang. Just to see. I first see your mother there.*

I think you know the rest of the story. My father was not the only one. Time pass. You go back there now to that kampung and still got some people here and there. Still got the graves. Tell you what, tomorrow we go. We go and find my father and I will show you. My mother also next to him although she many years later only pass away. Show you where got time pass.

Okay la. Think you tired also by now. You mau balik? Wait first la. We makan dulu. Got one nasi goreng nearby not bad. Wait for my daughter to come home—nanti she take you out on her motor. Then you tell me how you feel after that. Maybe that's how my mother father feel also. You tell me later how.

KAMUS

His shadow is large on the wall behind him. It flickers along with the flame in the kerosene lamp and he takes a deep breath, his pen poised above the paper. The smell of ink, of fresh paint. And woven through it, the fragrance of the night, sultry with the heaviness of flowers after rainfall. In the distance—although he cannot see it, he is aware of it—the sea presses against the shore, lifts away, presses again. There is music on a radio; again this is unseen, but it enters him, its poetry grappling with wind and moonlight, with the hum of electricity. And suddenly there is an ache that spreads along his shoulders, down his spine, into his wrists. He sighs and stands, straightens his body, closes his eyes, feels the liquid relief of the stretch through bone and muscle; although the ache is still present, it is replaced by an ache that is sweeter, languorous. He looks back down on the page. *Perdjuangan.* The Dutch *dj* like a doorjamb in the Malay, a stopper on his tongue. No—he bends over the page and writes next to it, his handwriting graceful. *Perjuangan.* There, he thinks—now, like a skein of silk, the rise and fall of the tongue straight after the *r*, bending into the *jua*. Now his heart is satisfied. It is time to head out into the night.

George Town is regaining its fervour after the war. There are lights in the window; there is music in the streets. Two Chinese women walk past him, their hair up in curls, their faces white with powder, their Western dresses swinging at their calves. He continues on his way until he reaches a door in a shophouse lot. A spray of light swinging around the raw cement stairwell, dangling from a naked bulb on a wire. He begins his climb up the stairwell—the ache has returned but he shakes it off—and he hears music as he ascends. He hears laughter. He hears a woman's laughter ringing above the low rumble of the men's.

When he reaches the landing he spies the source. It is Luqman's sister, a few months younger than him. Her lips are an impossible red, and her curls are hidden under a diaphanous veil that hides nothing, sparkles somehow, in the dim light. When she sees him she waves—with her fingers—and he inclines his head in recognition.

But the noise of the room distracts him, and he has a premonition of the inevitable route of the night—the arguments and the long, low talk. All of their throats turning hoarse, disagreeing with each other and turning inside-out whatever they *do* agree on so that they can find new threads to disagree with. He turns away from the crowd a moment, looking for a place to store his hat. The music he recognises, a popular song from Indonesia—it is a woman singing this time, her voice almost masculine, full of gravel and smoke, as sensuous as an animal moving through the depth of a night in the jungle. *Terang bulan—terang di pinggir kali—buaya timbul disangka-lah mati—*

'You've arrived.'

He looks up to see her, Luqman's sister. They are almost the same height, and he is already quite tall for a man. He straightens up a little more.

'Have you all eaten?'

'Luqman and I had dinner with our mother before we left the house. Have you?'

'Yes.'

Jangan percaya mulutnya lelaki—berani sumpah tapi takut mati. . . . They listen as the final notes fade away; the curl of music twines around the room, trails towards the window, slips away towards the sea. He sees her smiling and he cannot help but smile back, grudgingly. This is a familiar song, a beloved song. When their eyes meet, he has the sense that they are children again, sharing a secret.

Then the sound of chairs scraping in the centre of the room interrupts them—their cue to head over and join the meeting. He waves her ahead, deliberately sitting away from her so that he can participate fully without distraction. Tonight the subject is language; tonight the subject is revolution.

The news that night is about Indonesia. The continued struggle against Dutch imperialism, the continued revolution in the archipelago. Malaya lies within its cusp, in the embrace of the array of islands curving from west to east. After all, they are only brothers, little separating them but for a ship that came earlier or later, from a different part of Europe. When they talk about Indonesia, there is no argument. They are all clear on what they desire. The end of European rule. A land held in the arms of its own people. There is some talk that night of Malaya being the next frontier of the revolution, some of the Indonesian guard who saw their country as a second front from which to raise the banner of bangsa Melayu. *We speak the same language, after all.*

Afterwards, the talk turns to that very subject of language, the old argument—*in which language should the revolution be conducted?* The answer is always the same, but their methods vary, their ideas about language vary. Some call for eloquence, others for rough grace. But even some of the Chinese, or so they have heard, are partial to Malay—that Malay would be the language of revolution could not be contested.

The conversation stalls. Suddenly, Luqman's sister speaks.

'I want to bring someone to our next meeting,' she says.

'One woman more, one headache more,' someone says. The man next to him nods, murmurs.

'Don't worry,' she says. 'It is not a woman, it's a man.'

For God's sake, he thinks. Across from him, Luqman raises his eyebrows. A faint murmur rises in the room.

'And who is this man?' Luqman asks.

'Is he from Penang?' someone asks. 'I thought everyone we needed to know would be here already, working with us. Or perhaps he is from Perak or Pahang—we will have much to say to each other then, our brothers who are in the heart—'

'No,' she replies. 'He is from Penang. From this island. But you don't know him because he is Chinese.'

Now there is uproar in the room.

'Why, what's wrong? What's the problem?' she says. 'He writes also—for the Chinese press. I see no reason for all this tamasha from you all.'

'With a Chinese press? Kak, do you hear Chinese in this room now?'

'You people sit here, you talk amongst yourselves. After that? What do you think is going to happen?'

'This is ridiculous,' he murmurs and she looks up at him, her eyes bright. And he finds himself faltering, against his will, despite himself, so that he says—softly at first, then a little louder—

'Dah, dah—alright, alright. Let her bring him, let us see what this man has to say.'

The whole week the rain continues to fall; the whole week his bones continue to ache. At night the weather is frantic. Even between storms, the air is restless with the simmer of electricity, carried to and from the sea, from the hills in the distance. On nights like this he is brought back to the ripe smell of the prison, to the arrest which happened one afternoon as he was simply walking home after his Friday solat. The British convoy pulling up, the soldiers shouting his name. And him looking up at them and knowing that his time was up—all his talk of revolution, his campaigning in the streets, in the kampungs. And although he had always imagined this moment—always imagined he would be braver, be taken away with his head held high—the first emotion, the largest emotion, he felt was shame. His shame eclipsing even his terror. Shame that his neighbours would be seeing this, the makciks and pakciks who had seen him grow from boy to man, whose children he had played with when he himself was a child, whose kuih he had eaten, whose hands he had held in his to greet. *Some freedom fighter*, the soldier laughed as he twisted his arms behind his back, the heat in his joints matching that in his throat, in his cheeks.

Such are his nights. In the daytime he sits at the press he works in, dealing with the news. Rolls his eyes at the smiling faces of the European men, his fingers stained with the ink used to print them. His ears pressed to the radio for the developments in Indonesia—one kampung fortified, another fallen. He spends the evenings at a mamak, digging into roti telur, sipping his teh halia. The firecracker of ginger in the back of his throat. A kaleidoscope of languages around him—the burst of Hokkien and other Chinese dialects, some English, the ribbon-whirl of Tamil, the familiar music of his Malay. In the distance, the wind purling through the trees, carrying the scent of the sea.

On Friday they break for the afternoon solat. That evening he makes his way to the shophouse again.

He had hoped to be early, to settle himself before everyone else came. Unfortunately, on the landing he hears a woman's laughter again. Then something deeper—the laughter of an unfamiliar man. He stands there for a moment in shadow, massaging his temples. Then he straightens his back and makes his way up the stairs.

Of course—it's Luqman's sister and her Chinese fella. He is around the same height as her, with skin that has caught the sun and looking lean in Western dress, which he thinks impractical in this heat before remembering that he is also wearing the same thing. He takes off his jacket, removes his hat.

'This is Richard,' she says, breaking the silence, gesturing between them both. He is not sure whether an English name is worse than a Chinese one.

But Richard extends his hand, and he takes it. The handshake is sharp and curt; he does not move his own hand to his chest afterwards.

'Richard works at the . . .'

Richard breaks in, says the Chinese name of the paper.

'I am at *Berita*,' he replies.

'I make it a habit to read it,' Richard says. 'Particularly I enjoy the "Perjuangan" column.'

'I was the Indonesian correspondent for a while, just before the war. In Jakarta. My mother is Javanese.'

'You couldn't get away with any of that in the English daily.'

'What do you get up to in the Chinese one?'

For some reason they are speaking in English. Silence rises again, but luckily they are interrupted by the sound of voices from below—the rest of the men have started to arrive. He excuses himself, leaves her and Richard to face the others' judgement.

As predicted, they all lay into the newcomer. The interrogation is conducted in a strange mix of languages—some of the men use courtly Malay, some use English, others give in to bahasa pasar, as if the men here hadn't received a Western education, as if they go home each night to an attap roof, a clatter of wood. He watches her face grow steadily dark, but she does not jump in. Instead it is Richard who rises to the occasion. He volleys everything, all their implicit insults, as if they are speaking in pantun.

It is Luqman who breaks the sparring, speaking for the first time that night.

'Tell me simply,' he says. 'Why are you here, and why has my sister brought you here?'

'I met your sister at a reading,' Richard says, his voice sincere. In the dark, he shifts from watching Richard to watching Luqman's sister. She does not notice; her dark eyes are focused entirely on her guest. 'It was in English, but the writer wrote of a united Malaya. He was an Indian writer, from a plantation background. Inspired by what is happening in India.' Now Richard slips into Malay; his speech is soft, slightly awkward, but precise. 'He was not the most fluent in English, not like any of us in this room are. But he was stubborn. He made himself understood. There was an Englishwoman there, I don't know what she was expecting. But it didn't matter if she understood or not. She left early; the rest of us stayed. The rest of us understood. That was the important thing.'

Richard turns away from Luqman and looks at his sister. She is looking back at him too, and she is smiling.

After the meeting, Richard leaves first, a courtesy to allow them to discuss him. He watches her walk down with him to bid him farewell. When she comes back up the stairs, her face is set again, but her eyes are soft. He has seen that same look on her face many times.

'He would like to come next week,' she says.

Luqman sighs, looks around the silent room.

'Alright,' he says. 'For next week, at least, he can come.'

~

He sees her again at the waterfront. There are lights on a ship out at sea; he cannot tell what ship it is from this distance, in the deepening darkness. He is strolling along the promenade after work, thinking of what to eat for dinner. Then he sees her walking towards him from the opposite direction, her eyebrows raised.

'Where have you come from?' he says when they reach each other. The sound of children's laughter reaches them from somewhere along the promenade. The patter of feet, a dog barking.

'I was visiting my aunt.'

'Are you headed home?'

'Not yet—I was supposed to stay for dinner but . . . you know la, it's Kak Maryam . . . '

'Yes,' he says. 'I never liked her, I can tell you that now.'

'You had no problem telling me that then. Luqman says you still complain to him about her until now. Are you looking for food?'

'I was thinking satay . . . or a stingray, but it's ridiculous to have one alone.'

'I'll go with you,' she says. 'I'm hungry also.'

And so they begin walking away from the sea, into the heart of George Town. There is no need for them to speak to decide where to go; they remember the way still. They wend through the smell of char and fry, smoke rising from the large woks that appear in the evenings like strange animals. The clatter of music falls out of a radio-set, mingled with footsteps, the hint of the rain still heavy in the air.

Finally, they reach the stall. It is wedged into a lorong, low seats and tables scattered around an aluminium cart. Smoke thick in the air. They settle down at an empty table, and the makcik and her young son call out towards them, exchange greetings.

'So long, never see! So? Married already?'

'Oh, no—'

She laughs and lets him explain, which he does with some awkwardness.

'Well,' the makcik says, 'Life is long.'

He doesn't know what to say to that, so he smiles instead and places their order—satay kambing and a single grilled stingray, slathered with chilli and lime. The food arrives quickly, and they eat immediately, ravenously.

'So—' he says, 'How long have you known Richard?'

'Almost a year,' she replies. 'Yes, I managed to keep it a secret for this long.'

'Even from Luqman? You were always close.'

'Yes, but something like this . . . he wasn't happy when he heard.' She darts him a look, slides a chunk of meat clean off the skewer with her teeth. 'Not every man is someone he grew up with. But he'll have to get used to it.'

'Where did he go to school?'

'He spent his childhood here, but his father was from Ipoh, so he went back there for a while for secondary school. At St. Michael's and all the Angels. He went to England for university.'

'So he's one of the—what do they call it? The King's Chinese. An Anglican also.'

She ignores the first statement, saying only, 'He still believes. It was a faith he received from his father, who received it from his father.'

He pauses, lets the meat melt on his tongue; it is still sweet from the fire.

'The queen is the head of their church. I've heard the songs they sing.'

'He was working for the force during the war. He is fluent in Hokkien, Cantonese, Mandarin. In Ipoh he worked with the unions; he has his connections here in the jetties. You are sympathetic to the Chinese dockworkers down south, kan? To the plight of the workers who know the sea. He is not what you think.'

'You don't have to defend him. You yourself can't speak those languages also.'

'There is nothing to defend him from.'

'I'm asking only—will he convert for you?'

They are both looking at each other, through the faint haze that has risen in the lorong. The hills are behind her, darker against the last light in the sky, a mist rising from its jungles. But he is only looking at her. Only into the darkness of her eyes.

'No,' she says. 'Because I will not ask him to.'

'You know then that it cannot be done.'

'It can be done,' she says. 'If it is the will of God.'

If it is the will of God—that line sticks to his skull all through the days following. Grinds inside of him along with that arisen ache. In the daytime the press clatters around him, his fingers are smeared with ink. In the evenings he stares at the pages in front of him, the kamus he has been tasked to compile. The Indonesian leaflets on one side of his table—he will not take any inspiration from the European pamphlets or magazines—and a Tamil-English dictionary instead to his right. He contemplates the swoop of jawi in front of him, his gaze lingering. Then he curses, relents, and writes in romanised script next to it. He knows in his heart that the latter will be the better choice—knows that this is the script they all read.

His head is subsumed in thick heat. One night he chooses to do something to break free from it, calls on another woman he used to love, irregularly, dangerously. Now the second wife of some half-Arab trader, whose books are fat with the sale of fine carpets. He brings her to his flat, also above the press, so that the smell of ink pervades everything, and afterwards when she sits up from his bed the lights from the shophouses opposite are on her face, on her bare chest, striped against her neck.

In Indonesia, before the war, he had a Eurasian lover. Afterwards, in the fever of the revolution, her light eyes began to sicken him; they hid nothing, they were clear. She talked of her holidays in Leiden; she had a maid from Ambon, a little girl who liked to put flowers in her hair when she worked in the garden. And amidst this litany of women he had once loved, she rises again in his mind. Their childhood together, their shared language. She had been the first, then the third, and once he had wanted to make her the last. There is a picture somewhere in his flat of the two of them as children. He is standing to one side, Luqman on the other. She is holding a parasol and smiling, a gap where her front teeth should have been. Would be. *Even if it means turning away from God.* Even if it means being turned away from jannah? *You still don't understand?* He is *my jannah.*

Again when he sleeps he sees the stuttered light of the prison. He had been there with the rest of his brothers and they had kept themselves busy when they could, with their books and with their learning, with their language and their music. Luqman had been there too; they had made their promises there. That this was only a temporary shame, and they would again be free men, just as they would all be free—from Johor to Jakarta, from Kelantan to Kalimantan.

He rises from bed, shakes off the stale terror that was pressing on him, and returns to the kamus. He thinks of the word for *revolution*—even the Indonesians have retained the history of Europe within it. He thinks of something else to replace it but cannot; that history has already been written, has already become a part of them. The thread of history that cannot be denied. *Revolusi*, he writes, then falters over the explanation. He puts down the pen.

One day, he decides to visit the Chinese press. The *Nanyang* something or other. It is not too far from his own press, and he goes after his Friday solat, the sound of God still loud in his ears. He had last seen Richard at the meeting the previous week; he has become a regular attendee. Luqman had shaken his head, saying—*it is as God wills. If my sister brings him to the Almighty, then it will be grace.* He had changed the subject after that.

Now he stands in his prayer dress in front of the shop, hesitating. The street he is on is decidedly Chinese. Kopitiams serving pork, chilled beer. A man with a tiger crawling down his bare back. The perfume of incense from the ancestral shrines. He stands at the entrance for a moment, but then steels himself, enters.

The receptionist looks up at him. He sees the magazine that she now puts to the side, starlets from Hong Kong on the cover, the glossy paper carrying the gleam of their perms and the shine in their eyes.

He speaks to her in Malay.

'I would like to see a man—Richard. I believe he is a writer here?'

'He is editor for this newspaper,' she replies, in cautious Malay. 'Wait, please. I will go and find him now.'

She leaves him alone at the desk. Behind her desk is a shelf laden with golden pineapples and a small vase filled with paper flowers. Tacked on the wall is a rice-paper calendar, its page fluttering in the breeze coming in from outside. He hears a fire-burst of Hokkien from somewhere inside the office.

When she enters the room again, Richard is behind her, his eyebrows knitted in confusion.

'Do you have time,' he asks him, 'for some tea?'

They head to the nearest mamak. Already it is preparing for the evening crowd—the whirl and slap of chapatti on the flat stove behind them, the rapid talk of the men around them. He orders his teh halia; Richard has a glass of teh tarik.

They talk first of small things. Richard's speech in English is robust, yet his diction is precise and delicate. He thinks of the crowds—the Chinese and Indians—gathered at St. George's on Sundays not far from the water, the ringing of bells and the rise of hymns from the heart of the church. *For those in peril on the sea.* A faith brought to them by colonial ships. The orang putih vicar. Their talk continues. The various news reports that have come in from Indonesia, that they were also covering. News of the Emergency in Pahang—the communist soldiers—*soldiers*, Richard used, not *bandits*—a term he also abhors, thrown around the place as it is by the Mat Salleh. The warfare in the jungles. *They will not win*, Richard says, *simply because they understand nothing. How many decades have they been here?* He agrees with him. Their desire is something he understands.

A small silence afterwards. It is Richard who breaks it first.

'I know that you two loved each other once,' he says quietly. 'I know that you two grew up together. This is about her, isn't it?'

'Yes, but it's not like that. I have no desire to be with her again, this I promise you.' He laughs. 'We've had two chances; I've learnt my lesson. Too much has happened between us. It's not that.'

'Then, what is it?'

He does not know when they started speaking in Malay. At first their talk had been in English, but slowly, like ink seeping into paper, the Malay had crept in.

'Do you know what will happen if she leaves the faith?'

Richard clenches his jaw.

'She knows. I know.'

'Her family will disown her. She is close to Luqman—he will never speak to her again. It will be as if she were dead already.'

'She knows this. I know this.'

'All of us whom she had grown up with—to all of us, it will be as if she were dead.'

Silence.

'You know that when you enter Islam, you take on a new name, one that professes your faith. It is the opposite for one who renounces. In a way, she will lose her name.'

'I will still call her by her name. She will still be known by her name.'

'I have come to you because I know her; I know she might not have told you everything, the depth of what it would mean. The gravity of it. You do not understand what this means to us. Try, please, to understand what this means to us.'

This time, Richard does not respond. Instead he looks at him for a very long time. Until he sees his own face clearly in the reflection of his eyes. Then he begins to speak.

'The other day,' he says, 'I met an old friend. The son of the man who used to be my family's cook. We know each other well. For the past few months he was in Singapore, holding lessons at night. For the Chinese factory workers. Teaching them Malay. I come to your meetings and I speak in your language. We are here—whether you want us to be or not, whether you like it or not. What will it take for you to understand this? You are wrong—she *has* told me everything. There are many things that she has been preparing to lose. And when I speak in English, in Hokkien, in Mandarin, in the Cantonese I picked up while in Ipoh, I too hear the things that many others are prepared to lose. And the possibilities with which we must make our peace.'

He says nothing; he can think of nothing to say. Richard is speaking quietly, but his voice is tight—not with anger, but with something deeper than that.

'We should all be prepared for such a loss, for such a surrender. Because what we gain will outstrip all else. That is what I am prepared for. And she knows this; she believes this. Beyond anything else. Believe me—I am most prepared to lose. The possibility of that loss is the only thing I am sure of.'

They sit in silence after this. They drink their tea. Strangely, there is truly no malice between them after this, there is truly no anger. After a while, they begin talking about football. About the Penang team, the upcoming match with Johor. On this they are united. And some time after their drink has been finished it is Richard who rises first, and they shake hands in parting. He puts his hand to his chest afterwards, as Richard turns away to leave.

A few nights later, he dreams again of the afternoon of his arrest. He has made his Friday solat, is walking home from the masjid, still dressed in white. He notices the sudden silence on the street, blanketed by the thick heat of the day. He turns around to the sight of the convoy, the immediate knowledge that there is nowhere to run. He raises his hands. It is here that the dream ends. When he wakes, he lies in bed for a long time, staring at the creaking ceiling fan. Finally he rises and stretches from his bed, puts his face to the window to cool it. Somewhere he hears that old song: *terang bulan . . . terang di pinggir kali.* He makes his way to the desk, lights his lamp, moves through his papers until he comes to the blank box next to the word *revolusi.* He flexes his fingers, stretches out the aches and the dreams. Then he picks up his pen and begins to write.

CROSSING
THE BORDER

All day long he has had the television on. The news from Malaysia comes in garbled, through static, the news anchor's voice fading in and out, interspersed by the sounds of the world around him. Stray birdsong, the screech of a motorcar, children's distant laughter. He leaves it on as he moves through the day, preparing his scant breakfast—some bread and 3-in-1 coffee—sitting in the blistering heat of the afternoon and staring out the window.

In the early morning and evening as he putters about the garden, the television is swapped for a radio, which he brings outside with him so that he is patting the soil beneath the papaya tree as Malay wraps around its limbs. *Hidup Malaysia!* he hears. The predictions are being made, reportage from the polling stations. The names of the states read through like a litany—from down south in Johor to Penang in the north. Sabah and Sarawak to the east, over the sea.

He digs his hands deeper into the soil. They are spotted, veined—if one simply leafs through the landscape with their eyes, he would appear part of it so completely; he would be folded up neatly, disappearing into the earth.

Almost 70 percent of the voting turnout reached by 3 pm, he hears later, drinking a glass of warm water in the shade of his living room. Through the window comes the ringing of bells from the closest wat. There is a rice-paper calendar tacked to the wall of his kitchen. *9 May 2018.* Almost three decades since he has been home.

He does not remember when they crossed the Thai border because he had come through the jungle. What he remembers instead—the taste of earth in his mouth, the ripe scent of the soil around him. What he remembers—the sky a Krishna blue, the leaves around him turning dark, fading into the liquid mass of the night. *We are now in Thailand,* one of his comrades said, and he was so fatigued that he did not even think to ask how they could have known—how they could have read any borders in the midst of the jungle. So he had left his country, the land of his childhood and youth, for what would be the rest of his life—and he did not even know it. He did not think of it at all that first night in Thailand, once they had finally come to the safe house, out of the jungle for the first time in days. What he remembers—some old woman mopping his forehead with damp cloth, the smell of frying chicken and garlic. By the time the night was full he was in the grip of fever. It would take three days to subside, him drifting in and out of consciousness, until one day it broke and the world was clear around him. Birdsong that made the silence around him lonelier, more potent. Only then did he realise—cleanly and simply—what he had left behind.

At around nine that evening the votes are just starting to be counted. There is a map on the television, splitting the country into its various states and districts. The reportage is in English—the transmission for the Malay channel has been patchy, so he has had to switch channels. The Malay would have been easier to understand; for the English, he needs to concentrate. If he had been younger, he would have tried fiddling with the satellite, but he does not want to upend anything—does not want all the news to disappear just because he has moved an antenna an angle too steep. He tries to glean what he can from the pundit's slippery accent, which contains the echo of a Western education.

We are talking about the heartlands, he hears the commentator say. *We are talking of the hold that Najib still has over Johor.*

There is a kampung in Johor, bordering a pineapple plantation in the district of Batu Pahat. It is named after an island despite being nowhere near the sea. Pulau Bintang—endless acres of pineapple fields, distant mountains. His final memory of the place is of being alone at home. It is morning. His mother is visiting a neighbour; his sister is with a friend. His father is at work at the mechanic's where he should be too, but instead he is packing his bags, hesitating over a packet of biscuits on the table, which he eventually leaves behind. Instead, he is crossing the street in front of his house, moving past the ancestral shrines and their spiralling incense, the heap of oranges; instead he is moving through the music from the radios, some pop yeh-yeh twining into the still air. Instead he is marking his path into the jungle. On the fringe of jungle, nestled in the foot of a banyan tree, there is a shrine for a local Datuk, his black face obscured by incense smoke. He presses his palms in front of him, raises them to his lips, then his forehead. He closes his eyes, bows his head. All this he will leave behind when he enters the jungle.

Ten in the evening is when he usually prepares for bed. These days he cannot see too well in the dark, and at the same time the harsh fluorescent strips hurt his eyes, so he has no choice but to retire early and fall asleep amidst the chatter and hum of insects. But he cannot sleep tonight, and so he washes his face, puts on one of his good shirts. A button-down with a checked pattern. He will make his way to a kopitiam—not the one nearest to him but one a little farther up, in an even quieter part of town.

He knows that that is where they will all be tonight. The other exiles. The ones like him who had for years fought in the jungles, found themselves on the other side of the border when the war was over. Who are now without a nation, living on the fringe of the nation they had left behind for decades. He has not been there for some weeks. Not after the passing of one of his friends, whom he had first met in the jungle—that friend was a young man then, a fisherman's son from Penang. The funeral was Muslim; he had married a local woman in Thailand. His friend, who had sang their songs in the jungle about the absence of God, was shrouded in white cloth. He had never surrendered to the government but had somehow made that concession for a woman. In the last days of his life, he had started having dreams. *I am home*, he had said. *I am in Penang, by the sea. I can hear my mother calling even though I am far away from the shore. I can see the heap of fish on the other side of our sampan—we will eat them tonight, not all of them la, some we will sell, but my belly is already aching—I can already taste the fish, it is sweet—do you remember how fresh fish tastes, when it is just caught only, from the sea?*

Sometimes he hears Malay on the streets. They are very close after all. Penang a mere hour and a half away. There are many Thai-Malays among the locals; there are also the tourists who come up north. He has become used to the sing-song accent up here: their loghat, their lagu—like a lullaby.

In Kelantan too their Malay had that quality of music. For a few months they had put him out of the jungle there, pretending to be a newcomer, gathering information. The food up there had been sweet and sour, rich and tart. In contrast, one of his favourite foods from back home was nothing special—just ayam goreng soaked in sambal that was enough to shock you back to the earth after a heavy night. In Johor, he had spoken a harsh Malay that sometimes still resurfaces in his dreams, which brings back a name—the name that comes back to him now as he walks alone in the dark. But he pushes it away. The night around him is full of weight already, and his pulse has some electricity in it, charged by an energy rising from the south, across the border. He makes his way past the wat at the end of his street, past the reclining Buddha with the gleam of light sliding across his torso, his feet. Bells and incense. The chitter of the jungle around them. *Hidup!*—he thinks he hears, but he is wise enough not to turn around. Wise enough to know how porous the border between the past and present can be.

I grew up on the Causeway, between Singapore and JB, a voice on the radio says. *I was only fifteen around the time of 1MDB, I don't really know what was happening also. But I noticed the amount of people crossing the Causeway each day doubled, tripled. It began taking longer and longer for me to get home each night. I was fifteen, so a bit blur la—but now I know.*

—*Mak saya?*—says another voice—*of course lah, she will vote BN. Tapi it's easy la, kan? To blame the 'rural voters' or what, I don't know—but these lines, they were drawn way back, isn't it? You want me to sit here and talk about history? We'll be here all night, sayang—*

—*We work the tin mines, we work the plantations, we work the fields, and the British come here, and they take—no more!—Today we enter the jungles! Today we make this country our own! Who protected us during the war? Who left us to fend for ourselves? We only have each other—let us sing together! Tong zhi men—let us—I love Malaya!—I love this earth on which I have grown—which has fed me and which I also feed—I love—*

—*So okay la, you tell me what I'm supposed to do. My son I leave with my mother in Johor, weekends only I come home. I can earn more working in a kilang in Singapore than as a teacher in Malaysia, you tell me what I'm supposed to do.*

—*They killed my husband there—do you see—he was crossing the road, and the British saw a Chinese man, the jungle behind him, and they thought to themselves—he is a threat, he is a dangerous man—let me tell you now about his favourite bird, I have heard it sing every morning, all these years—*

—Together, together—raise your voices, my friends! My brothers, my sisters—I love—

The kopitiam, when he arrives, is full. All these faces he recognises. All these years between them, the memories they carry. He greets everyone as he looks for a space to sit. He finds a spot at a formica table. He orders teh tarik—they make it here the way he likes, heavy and sweet and thick. He wants that taste now, doesn't even bother to ask them to make it kurang manis. He is old enough that none of that matters.

The television stream here is clear.

'Any news of Johor?' he asks, his voice shaking in Mandarin.

'Johor Bahru? Ya, have—'

'No, no, there is this place—in Batu Pahat, Batu Pahat . . . called Pulau Bintang . . . very small only . . .'

'You sure anot, it's still there?' the lady sitting across from him asks. Her hair is grey and thin now, her eyes sharp in her face. There is a tremor in the hands he remembers once seeing wrapped around a gun, sure and steady. He remembers her from thirty years ago, when she was young, her beauty so bright it could shake an entire room. Her voice as clear as a river in speech and in song. There had been nothing between them, but to him now—with all this history behind them, within them—she is suddenly precious to him, he wants to pick up her withered hand, wants to put it to his heart, that is all.

'I don't know,' he replies. That is the only answer he can give.

~

Aminah. Some Thai in the blood—perhaps a grandfather. She had worn her hair loose. They were still young then. He had been buying some biscuits, and she had been standing at the counter of the kedai. A gleam of sweat in the hollow of her neck; it was warm, the sound of the azan for maghrib weaving through the evening. It wound through the trees, melted into the rivers, wrapped itself around their bodies, drawing them together when mere minutes ago they were strangers to each other. How long had it been since he had prayed to any god?

But there she was, and there he was also, and as he watched the light set on her skin, all he wanted to do was say a prayer in a language he did not yet know.

Aminah, he says and the lady in front of him sighs, reaches her hand out for his—

After all this time, she says to him. He inclines his head in reply, says, *Wherever she is now, whoever she is with—*

The woman who sits in front of him shakes her head. *Let it go, my dear,* she says. *All of that is only history.*

Once, in the jungle, he comes across a tiger.

There is blood on his hands already, there are tears in his eyes. He has been running through the undergrowth, has lost sight of his comrades. Then he slips on some stray twig and barrels down a slope, and just as he catches his breath, his balance, he smells its presence.

When he finally has the courage to look up, he sees it. The tiger standing between the dappled light that dissolves now into its pelt, into its animal eyes. For a moment, strangely, he is full of calm. Gone is the war around him, gone is the bloodshed he has witnessed, gone is all the clamour; gone is rhetoric, gone is the party, gone is the nation; gone is everything but for the tiger in front of him, but for the press of the jungle around him, and he is tired, he is spent, for years now he has been running—he pulls himself up so that he is kneeling, he puts his hands on the earth in front of him, prepares to bow his head. So it is finished now, he will become meat for this animal, so be it—he is tired, he has had enough—

They have been here for hours. Insects drive themselves to suicide against the fluorescents above them. All of them speaking over each other, the rest of the town asleep except for this knot of Malaysians who cannot return. The taste of condensed milk on his tongue.

They are the old communists. They have fought in the jungles, rallied on the fringes of kampungs, darted in and out of plantations. They have given their speeches in union meetings, written their poems on pamphlets, stood next to each other on the factory line. They understand that what is unfolding now on the television—no matter the outcome—will not be the victory they have desired. They understand this. It is no victory. The world that they have fought for—and, in some part of them, will always be fighting for—will not be realised by whatever outcome arises tonight. And yet what draws him here—this unspoken agreement that has drawn all of them here—is the simple desire for the land they have left behind: to hear that language spoken by someone aside from themselves, to catch a glimpse through the static of the places from which they have come; to close their eyes and hear the familiar rhythms and imagine another present, another future; to be as close as they can to the land from which they are separated from by a border, by the demands of history—

—And the memory of her hands on the back of his neck, the stain of light on her collarbones. How she tastes of the river. He is tracing his fingers against her skin. Valleys and ridges. Places to hide, to hold to the light. The room they are in is quiet, everyone is out for prayers, but she has spoken of a fever to her sisters and mother and aunts, and there is stray birdsong outside.

The elephant meat is tough on his tongue. All day it has been raining, and he is miserable, they are all miserable. No music can rouse them now, no speech. He thinks desperately of the fish soup his mother would make. Ikan patin, fresh from the rivers. A dash of pepper. He feels its warmth in his belly, desires it with the whole of his being. The rain continues to pour; it makes all the leaves above them, in all the trees, fold—the water endless around them. This mist, this light, this sweet heat that soaks the mind. He wants to go home, he thinks, with all the blood in his body. He wants to go home.

After three years in Thailand the language had still been brittle in his mouth—like twigs, like bird bones. They had signed the peace agreement, but until they renounced all that they believed—all that they had fought for, and all that their comrades had died for—they would not be allowed to return.

He was tempted once. Very deeply. He had been walking to the room he shared with another comrade, past a wat, and something about his own shadow on the gilded wall brought him back to Kelantan. The bells instead of the tinkle of gamelan, the shadow play of wayang kulit that could no longer be easily found. His head rang with that melody, that memory. Then he thought of his childhood, running through the pineapple plantations, his ankles bloody and raw afterwards, those blue mountains in the distance. And with everything in his body, he wanted to go home.

When he reached the house he closed his eyes, pressed his hands against them. How easy it would be. All he needed to do was sign a piece of paper. But the party—the movement—had given him language. It had given him power when all he had was desperation and desire. It had given him a language for his sorrow, for his love, for his grief, for his hope. It was this thought that stopped him. That made him push away the temptation that day. And again, for the day after that. And then the next day. And then the next. And then the one after that.

He is thinking about the last time he saw her. Aminah.

She was standing behind the counter at the kedai runcit, the light in the shop the same as it had been the day he had met her first, slipping against her skin, against the body that his had become so familiar with— that he knew as well as his own.

She looked up at him and smiled, and it took all the strength in him to walk towards her and say what he needed to say:

I have to go. Into the jungle. Sayang, I have to leave.

How many times, he wondered, have those words been uttered in such circumstances? Like a liturgy, a ritual. His only regret, one that he would spend a lifetime accounting for: that he lacked the ability to say all that he wanted to say to her in the language she had grown up in, that he was reduced to these mere lines.

But she looked at him, raised her chin. Her eyes were large and bright. She smiled at him.

I know, she said. There was a tremble in her voice, but that was all because she too understood—from the time she had spent with him, from her own understanding of this land and all the tides that had brought the two of them here, together. She knew what needed to happen. What must happen.

Go, she said. *Do what must be done.*

He is a young man, and he is looking at a newspaper in a shop. It tells him about the world beyond his town, a world that he knows nothing about. But a friend of his had told him about a meeting that would take place later that night. *For all the nights we go to sleep hungry*, he had said. *There is a world larger than this one, brother. All we have to do is seize it.*

That night he returns home to the sight of his mother massaging her hands in front of the flickering kerosene lamp. Her crooked, lumpy fingers, those eternal calluses. That night his sister goes without meat, putting into his bowl a bit of chicken that she has scrounged from a neighbour's coop. *You eat*, she says. *You are the one who is growing.* That night, his father does not come home.

That night, he leaves the house. Enters the meeting room—somewhere on the fringe of the town, just before the jungle. A small wooden hut, alive with light and song.

Together, together!—the man leading the meeting is saying. *I love—*

He can smell the earth, his head bowed towards it. The tiger in front of him.

Take me, he is saying, *take me now and end it, finish this—I am tired—I have fought for years now—I can never return—take me now, please. Finish this. Finish this.*

He opens his eyes. Straightens his back, turns around. The tiger is no longer there. He is alone, and the song of the jungle is quiet around him, its heartbeat matching his own.

They are so tired. They are too old to be up this late. But the results are still coming in, and despite himself he wants to hear the voices on the screen—no matter what they are saying—until there is nothing left to hear. Until all language dissolves into his dreams.

He is already on the border of sleep. His head is heavy. But then someone is nudging him, and when he wakes up and blinks he sees something on the television screen. It is footage of a young woman wearing white, standing at the edge of night, a few buildings around her, the sounds of joy in the background.

I am standing now in the tiny town of Pulau Bintang—

He straightens his back.

At the edge of the district of Batu Pahat in Johor—

And she is so young, this reporter. She is smiling, a big smile like she cannot help it. She throws her arm behind her—a theatrical movement that is familiar to him, which he has seen in so many recitals before. *Look for yourself,* the reporter is saying, and for the first time in so many years, in decades, he sees those familiar streets, those familiar buildings. He hears the laughter of these strangers with whom he shares a hometown, the hometown he has not seen for more than half his life. He hears their celebrations. He realises then that so many of the people he had once known—his mother and father and sister, the boys and girls he had grown up with—might be now dead or gone. He recognises nothing onscreen apart from his desire. A desire not for the world he sees on the television now, but the world that will be—in his mind—always on its way. And his hands are trembling in his lap.

How close he is to the border. How far he has been from home.

END NOTE

This collection is indebted to historical inquiry.

'The Light of God' was first published in the inaugural issue of *Practice, Research and Tangential Activities* (*PR&TA*). It aimed to respond to the theme of migration within a Southeast Asian context, though I have stretched the boundaries of geography and ideology as they would have been stretched during that period—and continue to be stretched today.

'The Request' was a story that came late in the collection, and which replaced another story that had depicted the life of a more famous figure. It was written to answer a question by one of my two editors, Kim, who while reading 'Kamus' asked—what was it that the Malay communists sacrificed? For a very brief historical explanation, I offer that the British declared that 'one dead Malay was worth seven or eight Chinese'. After the Emergency, with a dominant historical narrative written by those who declared it won, the Malay communists were faced with exclusion from their communities not just in life but in memory. For further reading, one may consult the memoirs of Abdullah CD of the 10th Regiment, Armand Azra bin Azlira's 'Producing the Subaltern: Epistemic Violence Against the Malay Left' in *Indonesia and the Malay World* (2023), and *Malaya: The Making of a Neo-Colony* (Spokesman, 1977) by Mohamed Amin and Malcolm Caldwell.

'The Exiles' was reconstructed from a patchwork of histories. The scene of the communist looking across the Johor Straits towards Singapore from Johor Bahru, one that is familiar to me, is keenly evoked in a film by Tan Pin Pin with the same thematic and historical concerns: *To Singapore with Love*. The story was first published in the seventh issue of *Prolit Magazine*, a literary magazine about money, work, and class.

'One Hundred Perumals' is based on the compilation of oral histories collected and produced by Dave Anthony, *Kaatu Perumal: Folk Hero of Sungai Siput* (Parti Sosialis Malaysia, 2015). Kaatu Perumal—and the context from which he arises, that of Tamil plantation labourers and their resistance against colonial occupation—is a real historical figure. He did indeed love football and is remembered for his grace on the pitch. Eduardo Galeano wrote most beautifully—with a hand unsurpassed since—about the sport and the place that it has in the heart of South America in *Football in Sun and Shadow* (Penguin, 2018).

'The Pawang and the Miner' is set during the Malayan Emergency—or the Anti-British National Liberation War—but the text from which it gets its inspiration analyses histories that stretch even further back. Teren Sevea's *Miracles and Material Life: Rice, Ore, Traps and Guns in Islamic Malaya* (Cambridge University Press, 2020) explores more deeply the spiritual ecology of colonial Malaya, taking a closer look at the intertwinement of labour and worship in the interactions between pawangs and the miners from China. Histories of such interactions challenge dominant narratives which claim singular ownership of nations and the stories that uphold their borders.

'Antipodal Points' draws from the spirit of liberation theology that emerged from Latin America during the 1960s. Gustavo Gutiérrez's *A Theology of*

Liberation (Orbis Books, 1988) was fundamental to the development of this movement, which also found resonance throughout Asia, particularly in the Philippines, where the rich and varied resistance to Marcos included a Catholic dimension. *A Theology of Liberation* was widely circulated among priests, nuns, and seminarians, some of whom answered its call. In recognition of that, I leave readers with a line from the late Father Gutiérrez—*love exists only among equals.*

'My Father's Country' focuses again on the rubber plantations that hollowed out the Malayan peninsula, and the Tamil labourers who worked them. The refrain of the folk songs that weave through this story, 'One Hundred Perumals', and 'Tashkent, 1968' were taken—and appropriated—from an article by Logeswary Arumugam and Kingston Pal Thamburaj. It is titled 'Maladaptive Behaviour of the Tamil Labourers during British Colonisation as Reflected in Malaysian Tamil Folk Songs', published in the *Imperial Journal of Interdisciplinary Research* (2017). I derived sensorial detail from the works of the late writer K. S. Maniam, to whom I am now repaying a literary debt. The story was first published—and commissioned—by the Asian American Writers' Workshop for their portfolio *The Rainforest Speaks: Reimagining the Malayan Emergency* in 2023.

'Tashkent, 1968' was inspired by the Parallel Cinema movement, which emerged out of West Bengal in the 1950s and sought to depict—with the unflinching and unsentimental eye of realism—sociopolitical conditions at the time. There was such a film festival, and it did take place in Tashkent, in 1968. I have tried to remain faithful to such details throughout the collection. With films from close to fifty countries across Asia and Africa being showcased, the festival was a platform for solidarities within the southern hemisphere to cohere. Meanwhile, I first found information on the 1941

Klang Strike on the Selliyal website, which had a post in 2021 commemorating the Strike's eightieth anniversary. It is titled '80th anniversary of Klang strikes by Rubber Estate Workers in 1941.'

The title of 'Atlantic City' refers to—of course—Bruce Springsteen's spectacular 1982 hit. At its heart is the Batang Kali Massacre, in which the British Army's Scots Guards killed twenty-four unarmed men on 12 December 1948. In December of 2015, the United Kingdom's Supreme Court ruled that the British government had no obligation to hold an inquiry into the killings as too much time had lapsed. There were many other such events throughout Malaya's history; the Batang Kali Massacre is only the most famous.

'Kamus' probed me in the process of its writing to think about questions of language, legacy, and liberation after reading Rachel Leow's *Taming Babel: Language in the Making of Malaysia* (Cambridge University Press, 2016). I wanted to know how love could persist within the confines of empire—where the languages, faiths, and histories we inhabit so often come into contention with each other. I did not know that that had been the question I was asking when I first wrote it. I have since found the answer.

There are a few stories that I have not traced to any text or origin in this note. These are: 'Returning North', 'Doghowl', 'Again, Through the Glass', and 'Crossing the Border'. Despite this, they all have historical underpinnings—their inspiration is the act of historical reconstruction and the roles of memory and desire in historicisation. I have tried to answer the question of how we might reconstruct a history when what is available to us is only a deliberately partial story, curated not by us but by those who oversaw us, who were adamant in seeing us in only one way and in getting us to see ourselves in that same way.

The answer to my question emerged in curious places—traces of desire in stray memories, out-of-focus photographs stained by light leaks, archival silence. The line about the weather in Hat Yai on the day the Peace Agreement was signed—*sultry and rain-sodden*—was retrieved from a newspaper article. I had already known the historical details: the dates, the locations, the actors. What I had been looking for, instead, were weather reports—to tell me how strong the light might have been that morning, how the earth might have smelled.

As a final note, I leave readers with the lines from 1 Corinthians 13:12 from which the title of 'Again, Through the Glass' was derived:

For now we see in a mirror dimly, but then face to face. Now I know in part; then shall I understand fully, even as I have been fully understood.

ACKNOWLEDGEMENTS

My thanks to the team at Gaudy Boy, particularly to my editors Kim and Michele, whose understanding and keen eyes have shaped this collection. They understood many of its key concerns before I did, and the book is stronger for the many hours they've poured into it. My thanks as well to Jee, for seeing the work through from beginning to end, and to Flora, for capturing the collection so acutely with her cover design. Thank you to my family for always supporting my love of history and writing, particularly to my mother and father who made everything possible. And thank you to Armand, for knowing what this is all about. To all other individuals whose perspectives and work have shaped this collection, who I am unable for various reasons to name—thank you, too. The dedication of this story is for us all.

PERMISSIONS

'The Light of God' was first published in *PR&TA*, Issue 1, 2021.

'The Exiles' was first published in *Prolit Magazine*, Issue 7, 2022.

'My Father's Country' was first published in *The Rainforest Speaks: Reimagining the Malayan Emergency*, part of the Asian American Writers' Workshop Transpacific Literary Project, 2023.

ABOUT THE AUTHOR

© Armand Azra

Sharmini Aphrodite was born in Kota Kinabalu, Sabah, and grew up in Johor Bahru. Her short stories and writing on literature, art, and history have appeared online and in print. She is the editor-in-chief of SUSPECT, a journal of Asian literature and art. She holds an MA in history from Nanyang Technological University and is currently pursuing a joint PhD in Southeast Asian studies (National University of Singapore) and history (King's College London). Her current academic project focuses on indige-neity, state-making, and more in twentieth-century Sabah, while her research interests include anticolonial movements, agricultural histories, orality, and the history of revolutionary Christianity in the Third World. *The Unrepentant* is her first longform work, and she is currently working on a novel that brings her back to Sabah.

From the Latin *gaudium*, meaning "joy," Gaudy Boy publishes books that delight readers with the various powers of art. The name is taken from the poem "Gaudy Turnout," by Singaporean poet Arthur Yap, about his time abroad in Leeds, the United Kingdom. Similarly inspired by such diasporic wanderings and migrations, Gaudy Boy brings literary works by authors of Asian heritage to the attention of an American audience and beyond. Established in 2018 as the imprint of the New York City–based literary nonprofit Singapore Unbound, we publish poetry, fiction, and literary nonfiction.

Visit our website at www.singaporeunbound.org/gaudyboy.

Poetry

Fablemaker: Poems
by Mandy Moe Pwint Tu

Eke: Poems
by Wahidah Tambee

Interrogation Records: Poems
by Jeddie Sophronius

Waking Up to the Pattern Left by a Snail Overnight: Poems
by Jim Pascual Agustin

Time Regime: Poems
by Jhani Randhawa

Object Permanence: Poems
by Nica Bengzon

Play for Time: Poems
by Paula Mendoza

Autobiography of Horse: A Poem
by Jenifer Sang Eun Park

The Experiment of the Tropics: Poems
by Lawrence Lacambra Ypil

Fiction and Nonfiction

The Unrepentant: Stories
by Sharmini Aphrodite

The Way You Want to Be Loved: Stories
by Aruni Kashyap

Lovelier, Lonelier: A Novel
by Daryl Qilin Yam

Bengal Hound: A Novel
by Rahad Abir

The Infinite Library and Other Stories
by Victor Fernando R. Ocampo

The Sweetest Fruits: A Novel
by Monique Truong

And the Walls Come Crumbling Down
by Tania De Rozario

The Foley Artist: Stories
by Ricco Villanueva Siasoco

Malay Sketches: Stories
by Alfian Sa'at

Other Series

New Singapore Poetries
edited by Marylyn Tan and Jee Leong Koh

Suspect: Volume 1, Year 1
edited by Jee Leong Koh

From Gaudy Boy Translates

Memorial Club: A Novel
by Mozid Mahmud

Picking off new shoots will not stop the spring:
Witness Poems and Essays from Burma/Myanmar 1988–2021
edited by Ko Ko Thett and Brian Haman

Amanat: Women's Writing from Kazakhstan
edited by Zaure Batayeva and Shelley Fairweather-Vega

Ulirát: Best Contemporary Stories in Translation from the Philippines
edited by Tilde Acuña, John Bengan, Daryll Delgado, Amado Anthony G.
Mendoza III, and Kristine Ong Muslim

Books by our other imprint, Bench Press

Sample and Loop: A Simple History of Singaporeans in America
by Jee Leong Koh

Snow at 5 PM: Translations of an Insignificant Japanese Poet
by Jee Leong Koh

Seven Studies for a Self-Portrait: Poems
by Jee Leong Koh

Equal to the Earth: Poems
by Jee Leong Koh

Lightly in the Good of Day: Poems
by Bob Hart

Try to Have Your Writing Make Sense:
The Quintessential PFFA Anthology: Poems
edited by Donna Smith and Howard Miller